A Thug's Story Not A Love Story 2:

Jacques and Zyyah

By: D'Ashanta

Table of Contents

Dedications:

First and foremost, I want to thank my Lord and Savior. Without you, I would be no one. To my Allure Me family, Mesh and Deshon, y'all mean the world to me, you have stuck by my side through a lot of things. Even when my own blood left me by the wayside, y'all picked me up and helped carry me on my way.

Magnificent seven: Jap, Blac, Keedie, My Guy Ty, Big E, Bodie, and Kamster words can't explain.

Wilner, Jade, Christina, Pammy, Krissy, Kee, TN, and my fans thank you for pushing me to the limits to stay in the game. We are definitely going places… see y'all at the top. MUAH.

R-Dub, love you son.

Rome: Bruh, you do the most, but you love all of us and you make sure you keep us in line. I love the drive you have to push through, you are a hustler and I have never met anyone of your caliber. We going places sis, the belief you have in all of us is unrealistic for people on the outside looking in, but we know who you are. S.T. In the building. I love you sis, you are the truth.

Dom: Your ass is a mess, but I can deal with you. Through everything, we are still solid. I want you to know that it's all love. Love you, boo.

Baby Girl: You inspire me to want to do better. I am watching the glow up, and every time I see your book cover or your link, it makes my heart melt. I am so proud of you. TT Des loves you, babes.

Ev: You know what it's hitting for. There isn't much that I can say without our ESP allowing you to already know. Bipolar ass bih, I love you though.

In Memory of:

Dontrell "Doc" Jackson

May 21, 1992 – December 7, 2015
Forever in my heart, thoughts, and prayers baby brother.

Synopsis

"Don't ever allow any man to determine your destiny." -Unknown

Jacques is a hot-head, known for blazing heat on anyone who crossed him during his uninhibited excursions of life. May it be a jack move to fatten his pockets, some fool testing his gangsta, or the husband of the many wives that he subjected himself to on numerous occasions, he will do what he has to in order to reign his throne.

After suffering a grave loss in the first installment, he had given up on life and all of the good things that the world had to offer. In the midst of a tempestuous moment, he meets Zyyah, an out-of-towner that knows nothing of him or his past, and may be the one to put all of the negativity suffered, into positive perspective.

Jacques, also known as Kez, will endure moments that he had not imagined in his lifetime, both negative and positive. The locals knew who he was and the devil that lied within his soul. He was always a mine, waiting to be stepped on to set off an explosion. With a new kid on the block, feathers will be ruffled, and tables will be shaken.

While on this unbridled ride of A Thug's Story Not a Love Story 2, you'll find out what happened to Jap and Chyna, while becoming emotionally invested in Jacques and Zyyah's astounding relationship.

POWKOW

"My ass, oh my ass!" Sin yelled in agony. He sounded just like Troy from the tv show Swamp People.

"Muthafucka, you got two seconds to tell her what she needs to know. You're going to tell her the truth about Ghladis, and you're going to let her know what happened to her moms, you dirty bitch!" I was livid and had had enough.

Kez, of all people, looked like he was in awe, stuck on stupid, while I handled business. It was like I had stepped outside of my body and watched the thug inside of me take over.

"Me bebe, ya gonna stand there and watch ya friend 'choot me?" Sin asked Chyna, who stood there with a face full of tears and a look of despair. She looked like she hadn't a clue to what was about to happen to her father. She resembled a deer in headlights, something was off. She had issues and so did I, but we were a match made in heaven... Or hell, I wasn't quite sure.

If it were my pops, I would have killed him a long time ago, I had been off the porch as far as street justice and crime. Chyna was naïve when it came to this life, being that she had been kept hidden from it all; It was Sin's best kept secret. Coincidentally, the same nigga she wanted dead was the same man that kept her out of the street life. Where they do that at?

4

"Did you say, my friend?" Chyna laughed angrily through tears. She held one of the scariest looks on her face that I had ever seen. "YOU killed my friend. Spare me the fake shit, you dirty bastard; you don't deserve to live. I wouldn't care if you died right here, right now, you heartless son of a bitch. Now I am going to ask you again," she stated, cocking her gun and pointed it at his member. "What happened to my mother? If you don't tell me the truth, it's lights out for you Pappi! Over the past few months, I waited for you to at least call and apologize. But you are so full of yourself that you never stopped to think about me or Ghi… or her parents!" Chyna cut me deep with the latter of her statement. This nigga was friends with Ghi's parents, he watched her grow up. With friends like him, who needed enemies?

At that point, I was ready to take his last breath. He took my girl's best friend, her sister, the only person she trusted with her all, and he was sitting here lying through his ugly ass teeth! He kept chewing that shit, and it looked like he wanted to spit. If he does, I'mma shoot his nasty-mouth-ass again! I couldn't stand there and take that, he was a cold-hearted snake, and he had to pay for his sins one way or the other.

"Look," I said as I grabbed the collar of his shirt and balled it in my hand. "Either you are going to spill it, or your brains are gonna be spilled all over the ground. I have had enough of your mind games!"

I was pissed because he was a piece of shit and he needed to let Chyna know what happened to Ghi, more so, her mother.

"Pappi, don't you think I deserve an explanation or at least some info to find momee?" Chyna pleaded. It was like the pleas fell on deaf ears. Sin seemed to be in another time zone! He sat there bleeding out, Chyna ran up to him placing the barrel of her gun to his temple. "What happened to momee, pappi?"

Again, he didn't say a word, so she pushed her gun harder into his temple. I guess she was tired and needed him to know that she was no longer playing with him.

After all that she had been through in the past year, she started to believe she was some kind of gangsta. I wouldn't take it to that level, but one thing I knew for sure, she was a damn beast with her pistol.

"Pow!"

We all turned and trained our guns on an unfamiliar woman with her piece pointed towards the sky and her free hand up in the air in surrender. I turned my head for a split second to see Sin. He looked as if he had seen a ghost. He was laying on the ground in agony as the beautiful older woman approached him with her pistol drawn on him as her target.

"I've been waiting twenty-three years for this moment, you dirty bastard. Tell her, tell her that you forced me to leave her!" she yelled with tears streaming down her face as she closed the gap between her and her victim, Sin.

Pappi stood tall and began to tell Chyna why Naomi left. Before he could get a word out, a heap of Cajuns came out with all kinds of guns. Handguns, shotguns, assault rifles, guns with knives on the end, and guns that looked like they had been around since the eighteen hundreds. Then the muthafuckas were wearing overalls, straw-hats, and moccasins. They were chewing tobacco and ready to kill a nigga on sight.

"Should I jest choot 'em, Sin?" the biggest of the crew asked, pointing his shotty in my face while I had my heat trained on him.

"Ne les tue pas, je veux juste expliquer. Mais s'ils tirent, tuez tout le monde sauf me bebe!" (Don't shoot them, I just want to explain. But if they shoot, kill everyone except my baby!) Sin spoke in more French than Cajun. I understood, being that I took five years of French, French was the native second language of New Orleans.

Looking over my shoulder, I saw the look of discernment in Chyna's eyes and the look of murder dancing in Kez's. I whistled to get his attention. Whenever he looked at me, I shook my head no, which told him to back down.

"You don't have to explain shit to me, just go with ya move Pappi," Chyna cried.

"Me bebe, you momee is a dirty mudda—"

"Just go!" Chyna screamed, cutting him off.

"Back down, les geaux. Don't come a lookin' for me, no. If ya do, me and my boys ya comin back in thousand-fold, ya hear me," he stared me, Kez, and Chyna's mom down. I believe his hatred for her ran much deeper than it did for me or Kez and Kez had stolen a grip of money from his ass.

"Come wit us, me bebe. I dunno if dese ya boys can protect you."

"I don't need protection, Pappi, I need to be loved. You know the emotion that you were so good at pretending to be capable of," Chyna said to him with tears falling from her eyes.

He looked at her with a tear threatening to fall from his murky green eyes. "Me love you more den me love anyone, Sha." That snake ass bastard was working her over. She took a few steps in his direction, causing me to gently grab her arm and pull her towards me.

Holding her tight, I spoke. "I got you babe, you don't have to deal with his antics." That, apparently broke the dam. Her weeping turned into the ugly cry, and I was ok with that. She no longer needed to be hurt. She's dealt with enough.

"So dats you choice, me bebe? Rememba dat Pappi love you, Sha."

"You don't love shit, you bastard," Chyna's mom spoke up.

"Chut up you drug-addicted whore, les geaux boys."

With that, him and the fucking swamp people left in the mud-riding trucks they pulled up in.

Chapter 1 - Ju'an

"Baby. Babe. Ju'an, wake up before you're late for work!" Chyna shook me awake with urgency. As loud as she was talking, I thought I was already late. *Why was I dreaming about our last encounter with Sin?* I thought. It had been almost a year since the incident took place in his backyard. That fateful day left Chyna's mother, Naomi, in her life, and allowed Sin's punk ass to escape, again.

After everything we'd been through I figured we were supposed to be together. I kept good on my promise to Ghi and stayed by Chyna's side. She truly wasn't the shell of a person that she pretended to be when we first met. Thank goodness, it was a façade. She actually has a soft core. I'm glad I got to know her, I almost didn't stick around because of her attitude. She had a privileged mentality.

"Baby, come sit on this dick real quick. I need to empty my nuts before I make my day," I suggested, trying to get some wake-up sex from my girlfriend.

"What you *need* to do is brush your teeth after you wake up! Your breakfast is getting cold. Get up, Sha!" Chyna low-key denied me.

I stood beside the bed and stretched my long frame. She tried to get around me to sit at her well-lit vanity, but failed, epically. I grabbed her around the waist and placed her body in front of mine, perfectly against my morning wood.

"Damn baby, you so soft with ya sexy ass," I whispered against her ear. She moaned slightly. Even with bad breath, she couldn't deny my electrifying touch.

"Stop Ju'an, I just got out of the shower. I'm trying to get ready for a meeting," she giggled. When she looked me in the eye then laid her head back, I knew that was my cue to keep going. "I- Don't- Have- Oh. Why you gotta be so- Oooh!" she tried to talk as I kissed her neck and rubbed her phat ass. Chyna moaned against my lips as my monster throbbed against her stomach.

Baby trembled but she still tried to fight me.

"I'mma need you to brush them teeth. The way that breath smells right now, you would probably give my girl gingivitis. Now move," she turned her nose up and hit me on my shoulder. I blew my breath in her face and we both laughed. I was not about to stop my groove to brush my teeth, Chyna was trippin'.

"Baby, take these off," I breathed into her ear and tugged at the waistline of the pink lace panties. They hugged her curves just right. "Let me tongue kiss *her* one time, since you don't wanna let me get my dick wet," I kissed Chyna's neck at the nape of hairline. I desperately tried to get her horny enough to let a nigga have some of that good stuff.

My tactics must've worked because I didn't have to repeat myself, Chyna came out of those underwear real quick. She laid on the bed, and spread eagle, giving me full access to her beautifully waxed slice of heaven. I stared at the beautiful sight like a thief to a diamond. Her peach was already dripping. I dove in, head first. I kissed, licked, and sucked her pearl tongue like it was my last meal. Chyna's legs began to shake, and I knew it was about to happen. I licked and sucked her swollen bud harder, then slid two fingers in and caressed her walls. That caused friction against her pearl tongue and made her squirm under pressure.

Chyna attempted to escape my tongue lashing, but I pulled my fingers out and grabbed her thick thighs. I held her legs in place and didn't allow her to move another inch. Within moments of her flight attempt, she was releasing her sweet juices into my awaiting mouth. I lapped them up like it was the protein I needed to get through the day.

Once she climaxed, she started reaching for me, and I lightly slapped her hands away. She relaxed, released, and reached for me again. I knew she had reached her height of euphoria. The slight tremor of her thighs and the uninhibited expression on her face, that I took notice of, told her story. While admiring her olive skin as it glistened, I thought about how much my life had changed and smiled. I locked eyes with my queen and wiped my hand down my face. Clearing it of any remnants of Chyna's morning glory, I stood to my feet.

"Baby, what are you doing? I need the *D*, come give it to me. Please!" Chyna begged desperately.

"You gotta get to that meeting, right?" I confirmed before leaving Chy there hot, craving for her pussy to be stuffed with my now semi-erect manhood. "That heat between your thighs comes from turning down daddy's dick. I'mma send you on your way like that, so you won't try that shit no more."

I grabbed my mans with both hands through the navy basketball shorts that I slept in, and headed towards her bathroom to take a shower.

"I guess I will clean myself up in the guest bathroom since you wanna be a tease. Thanks a lot, Ju'an," Chyna yelled through the bathroom door just as I stepped into the steamy running shower.

Moments later

I walked into the kitchen with eyes for my woman.

"I know you don't like your food warmed in the microwave so, I warmed it in the convection toaster oven while you were getting dressed." Chyna greeted me with a smile.

My boo is the shit, I thought before responding. "Thank you, baby. You look nice. I'm digging that color on you!" I informed Chyna of her beauty and gave her a temple kiss. Crimson was one of my favorite colors, had we stayed in Bama definitely would have been a part of the Roll Tide nation. Grabbing my plate, I sat at the kitchen island to inhale my breakfast before heading out. It didn't matter if I was at her house or mine, I always ate breakfast in a hurry. I think it was due to me always being late for school, who knew.

"Well good morning to you too, Ju'an, or Jap, or whatever you calling yourself today," Naomi greeted me with a scowl on her face.

She was such a beautiful looking woman. However, her attitude was horrible and unnecessary. Jacques thought she was trying to run me off, so she could juice Chyna out of her money. Truthfully, I had no control over what she did with her money, but would've liked her to stop allowing Naomi to use her. I guess she can't see it because she's just happy to be reunited after twenty some odd years.

"Oh, I didn't notice you sitting over there. I thought you found your own place by now," I paused to tame myself because I felt the rage building within me. I had to hit Naomi below the belt in an intelligent hood way. "Today, I will call myself Dr. Poirier, as will everyone I encounter. How should I greet you today, Naomi?" I returned with a slick grin on my face. The look in Chyna's eyes pleaded with me to be kind to her mom.

I'm not usually disrespectful to my elders but that woman has been on my ass. There aren't many people that I don't like, but she's one of the few. This witch is up to something! It's been barely a year and she's already gotten "help" with a car, a new wardrobe, and pocket money. I know Chyna has been funding her lil' party. She best enjoy it while she can.

Chapter 2 - Chyna

I sat in a meeting with new potential clients and couldn't think of anything besides the tongue lashing that Ju'an put on Miss Kitty this morning. Damn. He got me.

"Will that be a problem?" One of the two owners of GeauxMami.com asked.

The people that sat before me were up-and-coming web designers. They wanted to throw small parties quarterly, to celebrate their employees' birthdays and holidays alike. There would be several themes throughout the year, that would change with the season. I was always up to challenge myself, changing themes would keep my creative fire burning. Contracts brought in more money than individual parties did. Don't get me wrong, I didn't mind planning and hosting any size party. Fortunately, I was finally able to quit my part-time as my dad's accountant. I never talked about that job because everyone but Ghi, figured I was cut out for the family business. I had been keeping Pappi's books since I was sixteen and I hated it. Party planning was my livelihood, and I needed contracts to keep the bills paid.

"Sure, that's perfect. How would you like to proceed with the first party. Do you have a theme in mind or a color scheme?" I asked the couple who looked at each other and back at me.

"We don't know shit about parties. We are web designers, that's why we hired you to take care of everything, *Ms. Green.* You come highly recommended, I truly hope you don't disappoint," the dread-headed stud said. She sucked on her gold teeth as if she had food stuck and needed to floss. I looked at her and shook my head inwardly, I hated that disgusting sound. Quite frankly, I wanted to decline the contract and end the proposal meeting immediately due to her rudeness. Instead, we proceeded. For the monetary agreement plus the budget for each season, I was going to deal with her for as long as I could. The numbers would allow me to be extraordinarily creative, and potentially have clients requesting my services internationally. It wouldn't have been the first time I sold my soul to the devil.

"Please, call me Chyna. I'm sure you may have an idea of how you want your first party to flow, as far as schematics and themes. I will create the invitations, setup the décor, make the seating arrangements, provide hosts, servers, and bartenders, if alcohol will be served," I stated with confidence. I attempted to level the playing field before she took it too far and caused me to chin-check her ass real quick, rude bitch.

"Look Ms. Green, *Chyna* if you will, I would like for you to do the footwork for all of the parties. We'll provide the purse and you do your thing. You are the one with the niche for this. So stop talking and start doing, damn!"

My alter ego, Chy was knocking to come out. I'd never been confrontational, it's times like this I wish Ghi was here to fight my battle. She would've swallowed the bitch that sat before me whole and spit out her hair and bones. Nonetheless, thanks to Sin, the beast that lied dormant was awakened and ready for war.

"Babe, seriously? Did you have to talk to her like that? She asked a simple question," the beautiful bronzed-skinned, natural hair wearing partner finally spoke. As long as we've been here, I assumed she was a mute, being that she hadn't said a word.

"She's the muthafuckin' party planner, Shae. She's making me feel like we made the wrong choice by choosing her for the job. Judging by her work, I didn't think we had to hold her hand through it all. I mean c'mon nah, shit!" the stud enforced more rudely this time.

Oh, no this bitch didn't just sit there speaking to her partner about me like I wasn't present. "Um-um," I cleared my throat and stood up from my chair. "I didn't catch your name, Miss…" I probed as I stuck my hand out to shake the manly chick's hand.

"Joanie, but we aren't done!" she firmly stated as if I came to do business with her at her office.

"Oh, but we are definitely done. We have no business to finish, we haven't signed the contract that I had drawn up and I don't eat anyone's shit because it isn't tasty," I turned my nose up. "Therefore, I won't waste any more of either of our time," I confirmed and shook Shae's hand.

"So you're not going to take us on?" Joanie asked with bugged eyes. It was as if she was surprised by me not accepting their business.

"Unfortunately, Ms. Shae," I spoke directly to the femme, "I don't do disrespect. Although your offer is one that most wouldn't refuse, I will not be accepting your business proposal. As for you Ms. Joanie, I forgave your condescension the first time, thinking you would correct yourself after your partner gave you a stern look. But you didn't. For future reference I have an amazing website. My web designer asked for my vision, and from there it blossomed into what it is today. The same way I was attempting to get your vision. It was not a pleasure attempting to do business with you ladies. Ms. Shae, I truly hope you find a great planner, because your intentions are good," I walked them downstairs and to the exit, "Thank you ladies and good luck on your journey!" I fake smiled and held the door open for them.

"Fuck that bourgeois ass bitch, we don't need her. She ain't the only event planner in New Orleans. Talking about I'm rude, psst!" Joanie said. I winked my eye at her as she stared daggers at me and I returned her glare. That bitch didn't want to catch this fade, don't let the Sephora and manicured nails fool you. Just because I didn't fight, it doesn't mean I can't throw these hands.

"Maybe not babe, but she is the best in the south!" Shae replied, and sounded defeated. I felt sorry for her. Had she been the one doing the talking, we may have gotten somewhere.

Eleven forty-five a.m.

I picked up my personal cell phone to call my mother. She'd been back in my life for a little under a year.

"Hi Naomi, what are you up to? Do you want to grab lunch? I dismissed my prospective clients, so I finished up a little earlier than I expected," I spoke to my mother freely inside of the confines of my office. I had my phone on speaker while checking my emails on the desktop. "Who is that?" I asked as I heard shuffling and a muffled sound of a man in the background.

"Oh sure, I would love to do lunch today. Can we go to Copeland's? I am craving a juicy steak from there," she pretended not to hear me inquire about the man's voice in the background.

"Naomi, who's that in the background?" I queried again, wondering who the hell she had in my house.

"I'm at Winn-Dixie, Sha. I don't know any of these people," Naomi lied.

"Oh, ok, I didn't know that Winn-Dixie had televisions now. Anyways, I'm not gonna do this with you. What time do you want to meet and which location you want to go to?" I asked, dismissing the fact that she thought I didn't know that she had someone in my house. Tuh.

"Let's go to the one on Clearview Parkway in Metairie" she stated, as if I didn't know where Clearview or Copeland's was.

"Can you meet within the next hour?" I questioned. In the back of my mind, I knew she was preoccupied. I was no longer anyone's damn fool.

"What is that supposed to mean, Chyna-Sinc?" she replied offended. Tuh, the nerve.

"It means can you be there within the next hour, Naomi. That's all," I countered, in an attempt to diffuse the situation. I heard hostility building in her tone, she was looking to fight with me and I wasn't feeling it.

"Oh ok, I was just checking because you sound like you are questioning if I'm being truthful or not. I don't have anyone in your house, Chyna," she stated.

"Pressed, is what I'm not. I'm sure you don't have anyone in my house because you're at Winn-Dixie."

It was my turn to antagonize her mental state like she had attempted to do mine.

An hour and a half later

I walked into Copeland's to see Naomi wearing a fur hat and an oversized pea coat with matching fur trim. I knew it was cooling down, but the woman was doing too much. It was barely the end of October. And why did she still have that shit on inside? When she noticed me, she stood to wave me over to the table she was seated at like a scene in a movie. I smiled, but on the inside, I shook my head like, "really, don't you think I see your extra ass"?

I walked up and placed my cashmere coat on the back of my chair and seated myself. I noticed all of the appetizers and immediately my stomach began to growl. She had ordered all of my favorites, from seafood stuffed mushrooms to the famous crab stuffed beignets. There were at least five different house favorites at the center of the table.

"Hi, Naomi," I smiled and pulled the hand sanitizer from my purse.

"I figured that you'd be hungry and since I couldn't remember your usual order here, I decided to get enough appetizers to hold us over. You're awfully late to say that you rushed me to get here. What happened?" She asked and eyed me up and down like she wanted to say more.

"Well, not that I owe you an explanation on why I'm a half an hour late, but I was walking out of my office when the phone rang at my desk. Surprisingly, it was a player from the New Orleans Pelicans wanting to book me to host his birthday party in two months!" I stated, excited to share the news.

"Oh, you showed up late because you were booking a party?" she questioned dismissively, with her nose turned up and a wave of her hand.

"Well, yeah. It's my career, I'm an event planner. It's what I do for a living, book and plan parties, just in case you haven't noticed," I responded in a no-nonsense tone.

She acted like she was too good or something. Not to speak ill about her, but when I met her just under a year ago, she wore hand-me-downs and didn't have a dime to her name. I'm the one who bossed up her appearance. She sat on her jobless throne and looked down on me for being an event planner. The nerve!

"Waitress," she called out and grabbed the girl's arm that was walking past. "Child, I'm ready to place my order, please," she cut me off before I could continue with my rant. The waitress gave her a "get your damn hands off of me" look, and I giggled. Naomi was privileged to be so damn broke. "May I have Al's Favorite Filet, medium-rare please, with Parmesan-Crusted Tasso Mac and Cheese. Chyna, what will you have, Sha?"

"Hi, Zyyah," I greeted as I peeked at the beautiful, well-kept, thick waitress' nametag. "I will have a glass of La Crema, Sonoma Coast please," I requested.

I had a gut feeling that our lunch date would be one for the books. Naomi's food came to the table piping hot, and she ate while I drank in silence. I wasn't feeling her vibe. She started bad when she popped off on Ju'an at breakfast. I found it humorous because he shot her ass down with the Dr. Poirier comment. I smirked.

"What are you grinning about?" Naomi asked.

"Oh, I didn't know I was grinning. I was thinking about something. It's nothing that concerns you, *Mommy Dearest*, no worries," I replied with sauce (attitude).

"I'm not the slightest bit worried, tuh!" Using the cloth napkin that adorned her lap, she wiped the corners of her mouth free of any remnants. "Take care of the bill while I go to the bathroom," she commanded. That lady was a mess. I had no idea what her deal was, but she needed to tone it down. I knew that she was my mother, but she didn't know that I was still on the brink of forgiveness for her walking out on me, she had been making it harder with her antics.

"Public places have restrooms, not bathrooms, Naomi," I corrected. If her eyes were guns, I would've surely been dead. "Are you going to come back to the table before you head out or are you done?" I queried.

"I'm coming back to the table; I gotta get a doggy bag for the remains of my lunch and the appetizers that you didn't finish," she laughed and walked off in search of the restroom.

"May I get the check and some to-go plates for you, ma'am?" Zyyah asked as she approached the table seconds after Cruella Deville walked away.

"No Sha, you can split the check. I am unsure if she wants to-go plates or not," I smiled devilishly, and surprisingly, so did. She must've felt the tension between us at the table.

"How do you want the check split, ma'am?" Zyyah questioned with a raised eyebrow.

"I consumed the mushrooms, the beignets, and the wine," I confirmed.

"Would you like for me to take your card so that I can close your ticket?" Zyyah questioned as if she knew what my intentions were. I smiled and handed her my American Express card.

She returned rather quickly. I left her a very nice tip for being my silent partner in leaving Naomi to pay her own bill, for once. I headed towards my car and just as I made it to my vehicle, my phone alerted me of a text. Of course, I knew who it was from. I didn't care to know what it said but curiosity forced me to read the message. Against my better judgment, I pulled my phone from my handbag.

LLM: *You would walk out leaving me with this massive bill. You invited me to lunch, the least you could do was pay!!! (three frowny faces)*

I laughed at the message and didn't feel inclined to respond. I've been footing the bill since she showed back up into my life. I pulled off into the direction of the interstate ten east, in need of a nap. Oh, how I missed Ghi. It was sad that I didn't have any friends.

Chapter 3 - Kez

We sat at a corner table on the second floor that overlooked the busyness of my favorite gentleman's club, Che-Che's. I nursed a glass of Jameson and I couldn't help but think of Ghladis. I don't know why, but that night when she got shot up in front of me clouded my head often as hell. I think it was the fact that I couldn't save her. That shit made me lose a little bit of myself and I had been drinking senselessly.

We getting money,
We goin hard
She work hard for the money.
So hard for the money.
She work hard for the money, the gangstas treat her right, her right!"

Pastor Troy blared through the speakers. I sat, sunken into the hardness of the red and black couch.

"I can't concentrate on shit, my nigga. These hoes thick as hell off in this bitch," Fatts yelled to his cousin Kinrick. We were introduced to him as Kink by their grandpa, Dr. Hawkins, back at the hospital when Fatts was shot during the war between us and Sin.

He and his parents came down from Dallas for Christmas and from there, Fatts and Kink were tight as a blunt of loud (top of the line marijuana). The word was, he had a hardhead when he was a teenager. It reminded Dr. Hawkins of a knot he had to tie in college, that's where he got the nickname. It didn't make sense to me. But either way, that fool was wild as hell, and just as funny as Fatts, but country with it.

"May I get you another bottle?" The thick-bodied, caramel-skinned beauty asked. I looked at her and she continued to smile. She pointed her hand towards the table to make me aware that she was talm bout the empty Jameson bottle.

"Damn, she stacked!" Kink, Fatts' newfound counterpart, yelled over the loud music. Those niggas were enjoying the bottle service. But me, I was engulfed in my sorrows, drinking brown, and sulking. "Boss, you gonna answer lil' mama? She asked if you wanted another bottle!" Kink questioned.

"BOSS?" the long-weave wearing, dark-skinned, tattooed stripper gushed as she suddenly had eyes for only me.

Mighty damned funny the bitch hadn't looked my way until she heard the four letter word. I was fucked up but not too full of it to notice her money-hungry ass.

She made her way to me, salivating. She immediately started gyrating her stank pussy all over the leg of my black Balmain Jeans. Her ass smelled like sweat and thirst. I stared at her with a death threat ever-present on my face.

"Bitch, if you don't get ya trifling ass off of my lap and go take a shower. Man, I don't want your sweaty ass all over me!" I yelled, and Fatts fell into a fit of laughter like he was at Def Comedy Jam or some shit. She left looking like I had snatched all of her hopes and dreams. My face must've been scary as hell, because thickums the bottle girl, looked afraid of what I might say to her.

"Yeah boo, let me get another bottle, ya heard me!" I finally responded to the waiting waitress. She took note of my order and walked into the direction of the bar.

Within moments, she made it back to the table with a set-up of Jameson, some glasses, and a bucket of ice. I noticed her nametag this time around.

"Zyyah" I spoke over the loudness of the crowd. "I appreciate you not walking off and allowing a nigga time to order," I finished, and she smiled. It was as if the sun had come up in my section, if only temporarily. Her teeth were perfect as fuck. She was winning, I loved me a thick bitch with nice teeth.

"I was surprised to see you send Diamond away. She's every man's jewel!" she stated sarcastically. It was like we were aligned with the stars.

"Here's a little something for you. I don't like stank pussy bitches all in my lap. I'm disgusted that bitch assumed I wanted her funky, sweaty, community pussy in my presence," I replied with my lip curled up, ready to bust a nigga head, all because of her lil' thirsty antics. Zyyah did her thing, picked up her tip, and got away from the table. With all that was going on, I didn't notice a few niggas looking in our direction until one walked up to our section.

"Can I have one of y'all ashtrays?" the lanky dude dressed in Carolina blue questioned with a friendly look on his face.

"Fuck no nigga, all of the fuckin ashtrays round ya and you gonna come to our table and ask for one of ours. Nigga, if you don't get ya bitch ass away from here I'mma break my foot off in yo' ass! The fuck you think this is, a charity event!" I commanded, and held my place as the dominant nigga that I am. The dude started to walk off, and I guess Fatts felt slighted. There were three of us, true we each smoked either blunts or cigarettes, but there were four ashtrays.

"Here you go, bruh!" Friendly Fatts called to the outsider. I looked at him crazy as fuck. I wanted to murder his ass.

"Don't touch my muthafuckin ashtray, nigga!" I spat menacingly and stood from my seated position. He threw his hands up in surrender and returned to his table with the rest of the fuck-boy crew. I waited for them to look towards us, but they never did. I guess Slim knew not to try me, so he didn't say anything to anyone. Them boys didn't want no smoke.

I sat bobbing my head to the music and decided to head to the batr`um to relieve my bladder.

"Boss, where you headed off to, my nigga? You know we don't travel alone in these parts," Fatts queried as I stood to my feet. We were still in New Orleans East but there was always a mixed crowd.

"I'm scrait. I just gotta pee, my nigga. I'm never alone, you can believe that!" I replied and patted my left hip, which held my .45 caliber pistol, also known as my Forever Bitch. With that, I headed in the direction of the bat'rums. After I drained the main vein and was washing my hands, I noticed two niggas standing around, but I didn't pay them no attention. However, I was on alert, because that's how I was. I didn't trust nobody.

Just as I left, I saw dumb and dumber mean mugging me, so I prepared myself to get out of any potential harm. I would not meet my demise at the hands of a fuck boy. On top of that, I had never seen these fools a day in my life.

"My nigga, we got a problem?" The one wearing the red Polo muffled as he ran up on me, just as I made it out into the hallway. I was too lit to react as fast as I typically would've. By the time I realized what was going on, it was too late. So much for always being on alert. He placed his gun in the small of my back and pulled me back into the bat'rum.

He snatched my pistol before I had a chance to. Fuck! "Say, son, you know who you fuckin with?" I asked the young goon. He needed to understand that the little stunt he pulled had just signed his death certificate.

"Yeah, fuck ass nigga, I know who you is. You's a fuckin' old head that needs to retire on your own, or else I might have to force you!" he placed his pistol to my dome. I gotta say the lil' nigga had some nuts. He didn't even look like he was old enough to be up in the club. His accent told that he wasn't from the N.O. but his murky ass eyes was familiar as fuck ya heard me.

"Lil' titty-sucking ass nigga, you better fuckin' kill me right now," I spat calm fire. "I ain't scared of death bitch," I informed the soon-to-be dead man. We were nose-to-nose. I smelled the bitch in him, it caused me to laugh sadistically.

Red Polo growled, apparently getting himself upset. "Nigga, this could be your last breath. You should be thanking me for giving you a chance and not killing you. A nigga want you dead. Now, you got 30 days to get your punk ass niggas off my blocks," he grimaced, reminding me of my younger self.

I laughed agitatedly. "You can bet your life that I'mma kill you. Ya heard me, lil' bitch," I gritted my teeth. I wished the youngsta' would get my drift.

"Is that a threat, old man? Should I go home and get my granny to pray for my lost soul?" he laughed and looked over his shoulder at his homeboy.

I laughed the evilest laugh I had ever boasted from my gut. Red Polo matched my shit, then tapped the pistol against my head. I didn't flinch. I continued to smile at his lil' pussy ass.

"I don't make threats bitch, I make promises. I hope ya granny got that life insurance paid up, cuz you gone come up missing if you don't kill me," I spoke truthfully. No need for Red Polo to be misinformed.

BOK! He hit me with the butt of my own pistol. I didn't know how long I was out, maybe I was an old head. When I came to from the knockout blow, I placed my body against the wall between two sinks. I sat for a few seconds tryna catch my balance before I stood up. My head was throbbin'. I put my hand on my dome over my ear cuz my shit hurt like hell. I felt a warm gooey liquid ooze between my fingers, and knew I was bleeding from where the pistol had busted my head. That didn't stop me from looking at my hand to confirm. I noticed the watch I had on was missing. I knew they took everything else. I had fucked up, in a major way.

I grabbed hold of the sink and pulled myself to my feet. After another few seconds of standing and catching my composure, I stumbled out of the bat'rum into the adjoining hallway and made it to the opening of the club. Coincidentally, I ran into the bottle girl. "Oh my God, what happened to you?" she questioned. As soon as she realized my head was leaking, she wrapped my arm around her neck, and began to walk me towards my table.

Fatts was already headed towards us. "Big Foolie, what happened? Where the muthafuckas at?" he looked around pissed.

He scanned the club like he knew what the jack-boys looked like. If his ass did, them boys would've been the topic of the very next breaking news report. Fatts signaled for Kink to come over to help us. It was like the room cleared the way for him to make it to us unscathed. The music stopped, the crowd got quiet, then the lights went out.

Chapter 4 - Zyyah

Allowing my five-foot ten-inch, one hundred and seventy-eight-pound body to air dry from my shower, I sat at the foot of my bed in deep thought. After I allowed my body to dry, I lathered myself with cocoa butter lotion. I noticed my phone light up and stalked over to it. I had missed a call, so I decided to call back. The voice blared through the earpiece.

"What's this text message about some stranger's blood being all over you?" My best friend, Deja, asked through the speaker of my phone. We called each other every morning and talked about our previous day. I forgot I had sent the text the previous night until she mentioned it.

"Last night was crazy. I don't know what could've happened to this guy between the time I laid out his setup of Jameson, and finding him with his head bleeding on my way to the restroom, ten minutes later," I replied.

"Ooh, best friend, give me the chisme (gossip)!" Deja spoke in more of a Spanish accent than an English one. The bestie is bilingual and biracial. Her father's name is Dean. He's a very handsome, tall black man from Texas. He is the epitome of a man and a father, I love Uncle D.

Deja's mama's name is Jade. She's Chicano, American-born with Mexico-born parents. Tía (aunt) Jay was born and raised in Phoenix, AZ. We could always tell when she was upset, because she'd speak Spanish rapidly, and throw her hands around. Deja and I met in the second grade, we've been play-cousins ever since.

"You know how I am about public restrooms. The employee designated ones are trifling, and since there's restroom concierge in the one for the club goers, they are always cl—" I was cut short of finishing my statement.

"Sis, I don't care about how clean the damn restrooms were. Tell me about the mystery man and how you ended up with his blood all over your clothes," Deja cut me off, wanting to get straight to the chase. "You always do that crap, hell," she sounded pressed, upset even.

"Girl, bye. Tell me how you really feel," I laughed at her weak attempt at sounding interested in the events that took place.

"What? I honestly wanna know Bestie, and you're taking too long to get to the point," she responded sincerely.

"Your behind just wants to know how fine he was and if I got his number!" I retorted, which caused us both to laugh.

"I can't even argue with you mi hija (girl), cuz you might be right. However, my intentions are good," Deja responded between laughs.

"Well, unfortunately I didn't get his name or number since everything happened so fast," I stated.

"Lies. Bestie, you know your ass wouldn't have gotten his number anyway. Tuh!" De smacked her teeth. I ignored her truth about me and kept talking.

"All I know is his little homeboy kept referring to him as Fooey, or Foolie, or something like that," I replied confused. "However, I'm willing to bet that his chocolate self would have had you in his lap had you been there. He was tall and handsome, he looks like um, what's the tall dude's name from the New Orleans Pelicans?" I asked Deja.

"Bitch, that could be anybody. Hell, they're all tall as shit," she replied.

"I know right, I don't know why I used that reference." We both laughed again. "But for real sis, the one with the unibrow, he played in the last Barbershop movie."

"Oh, sis, A.D., yes that's bae!" Deja said all excited.

"A.D.? Hmmm, I don't think that's his name," I responded.

"I know, I'm from Phoenix. But we both know, I love everything about New Orleans. From the food to the culture. Most importantly, I love, love, love me some Anthony Davis. That tall drink of water can get it yesterday, today, and tomorrow. Um-um. I will have his babies and we both know I don't like kids," she admitted. It was as if she had dreamt of him wifing her up and impregnating her. "I'mma have to fly there soon as you find out who these mystery men are. I love me some New Orleans men," she said again, which told me that she was definitely going to be here soon.

"Well alright, Best, I will talk to you later. I'm actually going to go to the hospital to check on the mystery man. Since he bled all over my car and my work clothes, I deserve to at least find out if he's ok. Right?" I asked because I felt like a stalker.

"C'mon sis, if you don't stop doubting that you're doing the right thing and get to that hospital, one of the nurses may swoop in and steal your man!" Deja laughed at her own joke, which I didn't find funny. "I'm sorry Yah-Yah, you're so uptight. You need to loosen up a little. You left home eight months ago, it's time to get some dick play. I love you and I will talk to you tomorrow." With that, Deja hung up.

I grabbed my purse and headed towards the door. Stopping at the entryway, I took my cashmere button-down sweater from the coatrack and put it on, along with my scarf. The end of Fall, beginning of Winter here was beautiful, cool enough for sweaters. I was ecstatic to shop for the seasons. Phoenix had only two temperatures, hot and hotter. Fetching my keys from the keyholder, I exited my apartment and locked up. Once I made it to my car, I tuned into the music and pulled off into the direction of the hospital. It was located on Read Boulevard. Ironically, Marvin Sapp's *I Never Should Have Made It* happened to be playing. It's one of my favorite gospels, so of course, I turned up the volume. Coincidentally, this mystery man may have not made it to his homeboys had I not bumped into him last night at the club. He passed out as soon as we made it halfway to his corner table.

Pulling into an empty parking spot, I exited my vehicle. Checking my surroundings for present harm, I headed to the entrance. Yes, I got into the habit of that, because of all of the stories about how cutthroat this city was. Although, in the time that I'd been here, I'd been blessed because I never had any problems. The news here was scary though, so to remain humble and low-key unaware of the violence, I no longer tuned into the news channels. It didn't change the reality of children being murdered by other children, it just kept me from witnessing how often it happened.

As I entered the hospital, it was a stroke of luck that the two guys I helped from the club walked in. It was mere seconds before I made it to the information desk. There was a younger looking female in tow.

Honestly, what would I have said once I made it to the desk? I didn't know anything about the mystery man besides he was admitted around 2:00 a.m. through the emergency department. I was gonna just follow them to his room. It was weird that neither of them noticed me when I got on the elevator. I guess they were in their own worlds.

"Oh snap, lil' mama from the club. You left before we was able to say thank you last night," the shorter of the two chocolate men said as we exited. They were both very handsome men, now that I saw them in a different environment.

"Are you two brothers?" was the only question I had for them at the moment. They looked so much alike, but, I could tell the taller one was young. His youth was written in his face and demeanor.

"Nah, we are cousins, ya heard me. What are you doing here?" the taller one questioned my presence. The scowl on his face proved that he didn't trust me. I guess it was New Orleans, anyone could have cruel intentions, including females.

"I only came in to check on the guy that bled all over me last night. I don't know him, but, I felt inclined to know if he was well. The whole ordeal messed with my mental state all night last night," I responded, letting him know that my intentions were well.

He looked to the girl on his arm, then at the shorter guy, and he laughed like I had told a joke. "Where you from lil' one? That accent is killing me with your white sounding ass. Ahhhhh!" he laughed at his own ignorance.

I hated when people said I sound white. What the heck does that even mean? All of the strippers at the club said that, it really burned my biscuits. I am from the Midwest, our dialect of English is not broken.

"Just because I speak properly, doesn't mean I sound white, nor does it mean that I am any less black," I defended my culture of being a well-spoken black woman.

"Don't mind him, he's just a jokester. My name is LaToy," the female extended her arm to shake my hand and I accepted. Her make-up was beat to the gods, from the bronzer to the butterfly lashes. Her hair was very long and thick. It seemed to be her natural hair.

"Zyyah Hollins. Maybe it was a mistake coming here, I'll leave. I pray that your family member or friend has a safe and healthy recovery." With that, I spun on my heels and headed back towards the elevator.

LaToy grabbed my arm after trailing behind me for a few steps, "Zyyah, don't leave," I turned to look at her with an expression that told her to get her hand off of me. "My bad boo, I didn't mean to touch on you like that," she put her hands up in surrender.

"I'm sorry, but I don't have time to play childish games. The guy that's admitted here, stumbled out of the restroom at my job last night. It just so happened that I was also his bottle girl. He was injured, so I felt inclined to get him to safety," I shook my head for feeling the need to explain.

"Please don't explain to me chick, I think it's noble. Knowing those fools," LaToy pointed towards the two guys, "they probably think you're an adversary," she paused and looked at me. "I heard about you, its nice to put a name and face to my hero."

"An adversary? What do you mean? I don't know any of them. Why would I be involved with any of this foolishness? I'm not from here, I barely know anyone," I admitted honestly.

"I know that just by your accent, but that's how they think. They're boys. Anyways, the tall boy, his name is Fatts. We've been dating for eight months. I've been knowing him for almost a year now. The other boy is his cousin Kink, he's from

Texas. The boy in the hospital, his name is Kez, he got a concussion. His play brother Jap and his fiancée Chyna is gonna be here soon." She looked to the ceiling as if she were thinking. "You're probably right, you may want to come back later. He's in room 307," she winked her eye at me and headed back toward her boyfriend and his cousin.

Who said anything about coming back later? I thought. "Thank you for that tad bit of information but, I won't be needing it," I whispered to her back.

I resumed walking in the direction of the elevators. I was headed to the cafeteria to appease my growling stomach. Being that Sunday was my lazy day, I didn't want to stop for food on the way home, so, I figured I'd get it here.

Chapter 5- KEZ

Waking up in a damn hospital bed was confusing as fuck. Especially when I couldn't remember what the hell put me there. I kept trying to get up to go to the bat'rum, but those hoe ass nurses had an alarm set on my bed that would go off anytime it recognized I wasn't in it. The fuck kind of shit is that?

"Mr. Anderson, do you need something?" the cute lil' nurse asked me as soon as she came in to reset the bed alarm.

"Yeah lil' mama, I need to go to the bat'rum and get the fuck up outta ya, ya heard me? A nigga got shit to do," I responded as nicely as I could. I thought about that shit that Chyna said at Ghi's funeral, the shit about a year changing a person a lot. I couldn't help but think about how not much with me had changed. If anything had changed at all. A nigga gotta do better.

I tried to change, I truly did, but those fuck niggas always took me back to my element. I'm a thug nigga at heart, and it seemed I would get away from that mentality as soon as I fell in love. Neither of those revelations were realistic thoughts for a real nigga such as myself, so, I guess that'll be never. *Fuck I look like going legal and being in love? I'm Kez. Psst.* I thought.

"Mr. Anderson, you can't get out of bed and you shouldn't leave the premises," the nurse said.

"Say lil' mama, what ya name is? I don't think you understanding me right now, ya heard me," I queried.

"Kendranique is my name and keeping you healthy is what I do for a living," she stated and showed me her work badge.

"So you a RN, huh? That's yo real hair, shawty?" I asked. Looking at how long her hair was now in comparison to that lil' ass cookie bush she had on her work id badge. I highly doubt it was.

"Yes, I am a Registered Nurse and yes this is my hair. Although it's none of your business, I've been growing my hair for four years," she retorted with an attitude. "Look Mr. Anderson, ba-boo, you tryna live or die? Stretch out or be stretched out? Walk out or be carried out? C'mon, talk to me nah, I'm here to help you not hurt you," she looked at me crazy. "And don't be looking at my booty either Mr. Anderson."

This bitch must be bipolar or some shit, I thought.

"How you gone tell me you care about my health but get a lil' funky ass attitude over a question?" I asked and shook my head. "You know what, fuck all that dumb ass shit, man. I gotta use the bat'rum, ya heard me." Deciding to treat her ass like she was beneath me, I snapped back.

"Mr. Anderson, you have a urinal hanging here on your bed. The reason it is here is so that you may relieve your bladder without having to compromise your recovery by falling due to an imbalance. It's a known side-effect of your condition. You suffered a concussion, that is why we have you on fall risk." She must've realized she was fucking with a real nigga cuz she did lose the 'tude.

"Bruh, y'all got a piss jug hanging on my bed? What kind of fuckin' establishment this is, my nigga? Piss is biohazardous waste. I don't care if it is my piss!" I retorted in disgust. "Man, if you d—"

"What up, Big Foolie?" Fatts asked as he rounded the corner and checked the nurse that I was arguing with, using his eyes only. That nigga walked in like he was Barack Obama or some shit.

"Lil' one, do you knock?" I was feeling some type of way because he cut my rant short, I had to question his manners.

"Nah, not when I hear commotion on the other side of the door, I don't. I had to make sure you were safe. It's my fault you in this room now. I allowed you to tell me you were good enough to go to the restroom by yourself last night. I knew better but I didn't want you snapping on me," the look on his face made me know that he truly felt bad. I couldn't remember shit from last night, all I could do was take the word of the people who were with me.

"Hey Kez." LaToy spoke. At one point, I didn't like her lil' ass. I thought she was hot in the pants and after Fatts' money. So far, she has proved me wrong. I'm proud of baby girl, she graduated high school and started at Dillard University. Plus, last year she could've walked out on my guy, but she stuck by his side through all the tragic events.

"What's up, baby girl. Fatts treating you right, lil' mama?" I responded.

"Yeah, he is," she replied.

"That's because he knows I will fuck his ass up if he don't," we all laughed.

"Ahem" someone cleared their thoak. "Excuse me, Mr. Anderson, do you still wanna use the restroom?" Kendranique asked.

"My bad, mean ass. I forgot you were in here once the fam showed up. Nah, I don't wanna piss in a urinal in a room full of people. I will hold it, thanks." Not feeling the idea of public urination, I had to politely ask her ass to dismiss herself.

"I had no intentions on giving you the urinal to use, I was going to assist you to the restroom, sir. Hit your call button if you need us," she replied and exited before I could tell her to take me.

"Damn! Shawty thick as hell, mane, and she's a nurse. T. Jones would love her. Ahh!" Kink, goofier than Fatts, laughed at his own reference of the nurse. Being around him, I learned that Dallas niggas called their mom T. Jones.

"Man, you wild as fuck. What y'all niggas doing up here? Y'all must be coming break me out this bitch so we can go sleep these fuck ass niggas."

"What fuck ass niggas? That's the problem bro, you need to slow your ass down. You have a concussion, give yourself some time to heal, man," Jap's voice hit the corner, coming into the openness of the room before he did.

"Here we go with the holier than thou shit. Cut a nigga some slack man, fuck. Dude gave me a concussion. If you halfway believe this fuck-boy gone walk free, you got me fucked up worse than he do, shid!" I had to be clear.

"Bruh, stop trippin'. You know what it's hitting for. Just like I hit that corner without you knowing I was there, it could've been the swine. Taking notes and waiting in the shadows to catch you slipping," Jap's rebuttal made me kick myself in the ass. He had been ride or die all of our lives, and after what took place last night, I knew he meant well.

"Yo, you right my nigga," was all I could say. As simple as it seemed, that agreement cleared the air that could've gotten thick. Unbeknownst to any of them, the pigs had already been up here, I'm surprised nobody smelled the bacon.

"Ok, is y'all mufuckas finished or is y'all done?" Kink asked in a thick Dallas accent. That statement caused all of us to laugh.

"Nigga, what is so important that you felt the need to butt into our argument, ya heard me?" I asked Kink. I knew he knew not to get into our squabbles, so with that knowledge, I also knew he had to have something to say.

"Ol' girl from last night came up here and cuz ran her off," Kink said.

"Why you being messy like them hoes, bruh?" Fatts responded in defense.

"Ha. You did run her off, baby. She looked pretty hurt about it too," Toy chimed in.

"Damn bae, who side you on? You just gone throw me under the bus like that over somebody you barely know," Fatts turned on LaToy.

"Who is ol' girl from last night?" Jap chimed in with Chyna tuned in like she was watching a tennis match. She looked from me to Kink and back to me.

"Why you looking all crazy, sis? I don't know who they talm bout so don't go being Chuck Woolery. This is not *The Love Connection*." Knowing Chy always want a nigga to be in love and shit, I had to go on and shut that shit down. Early, not late on her ass.

"Man, shawty was thick as fuck. I don't understand how you don't remember. I guess you won't find out because somebody ran her off. I ain't saying no names, Fatts." Kink's silly ass called out Fatts anyway. "Boss man, as much as you drooled over her last night, I fell back. Now, I feel some type of way cuz you don't even remember lil' mama. Ahhhh!" he laughed.

"Shit nigga, I can't remember hardly nothing. I was washing my hands then got bust in the damn head. I can't picture his face yet, but I know he had on a red shirt and some familiar ass eyes. Oh, and he threatened to take me out the game of life if I didn't clear my blocks, so he can take over saying somebody wanted me dead but he was sparing me." Informing my people of how fucked up I was, made me realize that I had been fucking up. I had been drinking way too much lately. I needed to fix that shit and fast.

The room was quiet, I guess everyone was in think mode. Including the girls, we don't need either of them involved in this shit.

"Knock, knock," the familiar voice of my *favorite* nurse, Kendranique, sang and broke the silence. "Mr. Anderson, it's time for your meds," she smiled.

Is this bitch schizophrenic, suffering from multiple personality disorder, or something? I thought to myself. "Sis, can you watch her? I don't trust her ass. She just left out of here ready to take my head off, now she smiling, talm about it's time to give me medicine and shit. Matter of fact, what you giving me? I'm about to Google that shit. Let me see them pills," they laughed but I didn't find shit funny. Neither did Chyna, I guess she saw the seriousness in my face.

"Bro, do you really think this lady will risk her job, and her freedom, by giving you the wrong meds?" Jap asked, pissing me the fuck off.

"My nigga, you wasn't here when she was in here snapping. I don't expect you to understand, *Dr. Poirier*. Fellas, tell this fool how she was treating me cuz I didn't wanna piss in a bottle in front y'all."

"Mr. Anderson, let's be honest. I didn't try to make you urinate in the presence of your visitors. I was trying to get you to understand the dangers of being out of bed. You are a fall risk due to the concussion and you had gotten up, causing your bed alarm to alert the nurse's station. When I came into the room to have you urinate in the urinal, no one was here. Am I right?" Kendra corrected me. I couldn't stand her sexy, all natural ass.

"No disrespect Kendranique, but if my brother doesn't trust you, I gotta take his word for it. He protects me with his life, therefore, it's only fair that I protect him with mine," Chyna spoke up before I could respond to her smot-mouf (smart-mouth) ass.

"Ooop!" LaToy couldn't help her pettiness. We all looked at her, her retarded ass looked at the ceiling, like we didn't know she was the culprit.

"Mr. Anderson, I assure you that I love my job just as much as I love my freedom. I wouldn't da—" Her spiel was cut short.

"Yeah, yeah, yeah. Where are the meds that you are about to dispense?" Chyna wasn't playing with her ass. We all smirked while Jap sat there seething. Regardless to how he felt, sis got the job done. I signed for Chy to become my proxy and she handled everything. I took my meds upon Chy giving me the go ahead. The fellas dapped me up and the ladies gave me a kiss on the cheek and they exited. Left to succumb to the drowsiness of the drug, I fell into a deep slumber and immediately started to dream.

"Jacques Pierre Anderson, if you don't get your narrow ass in here and take a shower I'mma beat the black off of you boy," mama yelled from the screened in porch."

"I'm coming mama, dang." I spat, mad that I had to leave. "I will see you tomorrow bro, are we walking to school in the morning or is Pops taking us?" I asked Jap.

"You know his ass is taking us. He is scared that the dope boys are gonna reel us in because of their fancy cars and flashy jewelry." Jap complained.

I wished I had a dad. Momma was the neighborhood whore, she fucked any man that was willing to break bread. She was never home, but I knew what she was doing when she wasn't there and so did all of the kids at my school.

Even though we were seventh graders, kids were some bitches. They teased me about my mother but my mother only gave me the best of everything. Clothes, shoes, jewelry, and food.

"Did you hear me?" Jap asked

"Nah, what did you say?" I replied.

"I said, it's ok man, I saw the look in your eye, at least you have a mom, I don't even remember mine anymore. She only wants the best for you." He hugged my neck as we walked towards our house. We lived in a duplex attached to each other.

As I stepped on the porch, I recognized the 'fuck em'
dress mama had on and knew that tonight would be
another lonely night.

"Kezzy, mama is going to see a man about a dog. When I
get home, I will have something nice for you, ok?" she
assured me as she always did.

"Yes ma'am," I responded. I wanted to ask to sleep at
Jap's but because it was a school night I already knew the
answer would be no.

I ended up watching B.E.T. until I fell asleep. Before long,
mama woke me up for school.

"Mama, what happened to you?" I inquired about the
busted-lip and the black-eye she had.

"I fucked with the wrong person's money baby, go bathe
for school." Was all she said.

I got into the shower and had a blackout. When I came to,
the bathroom was ripped to pieces and there were strange
people standing there with my mama, who was crying her
eyes out. One of them held white a coat with all kinds of
silver buckles on it. They put it on me and took me to a
white van parked in front of our house. We got in and I
took notice of the time, it was 11:52 a.m. They drove me
to the Children's Hospital and checked me into the
Mental Ward.

I don't know why I woke up at that exact moment, but
I'm glad I did. Thank God, I was just dreaming and it wasn't the

actual day that I found out I had Manic Schizoaffective Disorder or Schizophrenia. After all of the years, it was still unclear.

Looking around my room, I recognized the back of a thick female in street clothes walking towards the door.

"Who the fuck is you?" I managed to ask in a raspy tone before she made her exit.

Returning with the brightest smile I had been graced with, she spoke. "Hi, don't you remember me? We spoke briefly at the club last night." Immediately, I felt uneasy.

"How the fuck did you know I was here and why are you here?" I asked grabbing my pistol that I had Fatts bring up here today, and placing it in my lap. I questioned her motive.

The stranger's eyes grew big as silver dollars. "Whoa, why do you have a gun in your hospital room? I am Zyyah, I was your bottle girl last night and you ran into me with your head bleeding when I was on my way to the restroom," she spoke breathily. It was as if she was afraid, and the bitch had every right to be.

"Again." *Click!* I cocked my gun and stared her down like the enemy that she could possibly be. "How the fuck did you know I was here, Lil' Mama? Ya heard me," I finished my question with a deadly scowl.

"Again," she mocked me, not realizing the danger she had put herself in. I hated when a bitch made a mockery of me. "We exchanged a few jokes in reference to the thirsty stripper while I was serving your drinks. Moments later, you ran into me when you turned the corner from the restrooms. I got you to your guy friends, they needed help getting you to the hospital because you had passed out. They mentioned something about your truck being too high to put you into because y'all rode together, so, I volunteered to help. I had to have my car cleaned because you bled all over it. That's neither here nor there, because I could've very well said no." It looked like she tried to hold her tears back.

"I felt the need to come here to make sure you were ok. Needless to say, all of this was a mistake. Have a safe and healthy recovery, I am so out of here. I don't need this, I didn't sign up for another interrogation." This chick sounded so damn white, I couldn't take her serious.

"Say Lil' Mama, where you from and who interrogated you?" managed to escape my voice box. I was curious as to which detectives had questioned her, so I had to ask before she had a chance to leave.

She stopped in her tracks, "First of all my name isn't Lil' Mama, it's Zyyah. You should've asked all the questions you wanted to ask before treating me like your freaking enemy. I don't know you and I don't know who did this to you," she proceeded to exit.

Little did she know, I'mma find her ass and make her talk to me. Her defiance made my dick hard.

Chapter 6- Ju'an

A month later…

"Damn baby, you must be trying to get us pregnant," Chyna panted into my chest after I had emptied my nuts inside of her.

"Not really, but if I keep filling you with my seeds it will happen, love," I responded as I played in her hair. I loved playing in her hair, not only because it was her natural hair, but because I liked to pull it. It was crazy to watch it recoil to its original form, when it was in its natural state. I know it's corny, but it's the finer things in life that keeps me happy.

"I gotta take a shower, baby. I love laying in the bliss of our sex-capades but I love a clean body, and my eyes are getting heavy. It's been a long week, I've been beat. For some apparent reason, my back has been aching like crazy," Chyna whined, like a kid getting ready for school.

"Next week will be better, love. I have a new patient tomorrow, he has the most unique name for a man. I pray he's been taking care of his hygiene since he's only nineteen," I rebutted.

"You're right, baby. Monday is a new day, a new work week. I claim a great week ahead of us. I will book the next six months of parties this week and you will have a week of new patients that will be loyal."

My eyes were pretty heavy themselves. I hopped in the hall shower, since we were at my house. I kept both bathrooms stocked for me, I liked to have variety. Speaking of which, the hall bathroom had Tom Ford. It's a win for me, and the smell of it relaxed me, causing me to sleep well. I scrubbed down and was asleep before Chyna made it out. With her long shower taking ass.

$$$$

"Damn, I overslept baby!" Chyna griped. I noticed that she had been cussing a lot lately. I shrugged it off and continued to brush my hair.

"I woke you up bae, you said your meeting was at ten and to leave you alone because you had your alarm set. I left your ass alone because I know how you get when you wanna sleep. I didn't want to have to D.D.T. your ass. Ha, Ha," I laughed.

"You come try it, and see don't I put you in a headlock, and sit on your face. Ha, Ha," she laughed at her own joke.

You've also been horny. That's why your ass overslept, we had sex three times, I smiled in thought,

"Baby, what's up with you?" I queried, wondering where this onset horniness came into play.

"What do you mean, Ju'an?" Chyna looked as confused as she sounded.

"I'm not complaining, but where is all this horniness coming from? Trust me, I love that good stuff. I'm just wondering if it will affect us in the future," I advised her of my observation.

"Babe, are you tired of having sex with me? We have barely been together a year and you're already tired of me?" Sniffles filled the air, catching my attention.

I briskly walked over to her from the dresser where I stood, and took her into my arms. Holding her there, I kissed away her tears and allowed her to feel my presence.

"Baby, I ain't going nowhere, stop tripping. And why are you crying boo, it was just an observation. That good stuff will never get old," I kissed her lips and laid in bed with her.

Sliding my hand inside of her panties, damn, she was leaking. I just wanted to play with it to make her know that I wasn't going anywhere. It was so wet I decided to lick my fingers. "Damn them pussy juices taste good baby, take them damn panties off so I can show you something."

Doing as she was told, I stripped down to my wife-beater and dove in that pussy like I was Michael Phelps.

$$$$

"Dr. Poirier?" My front desk questioned, in a pleasurable tone.

"Yes, Mrs. Rose?" I replied to my sixty-one-year-old secretary.

"Your 10:45 is here. Should I have him setup in room three?"

Adjusting my black onyx and diamond cuff links, I responded, "Yes ma'am, I'll be in shortly."

Mrs. Rose doesn't like me to call her ma'am at work. I wouldn't address her any other way, my Pops raised me like that. I adjusted my tie in the mirror and headed out of my office toward the exam room. Yes, I have a mirror in my office. What can I say, I'm a pretty boy. But don't confuse me with being narcissistic.

Knock. Knock. I entered exam three. "Good morning, I'm Dr. Poirier," I extended my arm to shake the hand of the young man that sat on the exam table. "How's it going?"

"I'm aight Doc. Today is a great day, ya heard me, I'm getting my teeth cleaned and I finally get to meet you." Throwing me for a loop with the latter of his statement, I didn't show any inkling, just continued to smile and keep it moving. "You look pretty young to be a dentist," he continued to make small talk. He apparently felt the tension building.

"I'll be twenty-four next Sunday. Sit back for me, I'm going to lay this chair back, so we can get started." His murky green eyes look just like Sin's punk ass eyes. I kept checking this cat out throughout the exam. The way he was eyeballing me, he made me feel uncomfortable in my skin, but I worked through it. I pulled my overhead light down and got to work. "Eight, fourteen, twenty-three," I called out the teeth that needed x-rays to my dental assistant, Tarsha and she circled them on her pad.

I let the chair up and removed his shirt protector. He stared at Tarsha's ass as she prepped the x-ray machine.

"You fucking that ain't you, Doc?" he asked in a hushed tone without looking at me.

"Nah, man. I have an old lady, and even if I didn't, I know better than to mix business with pleasure," I responded, ensuring that he knew that she was free range. With that, I left the exam room so that Tarsha could do her thing with the black and whites and then the hygienist could do her thing getting his teeth scraped clean.

I sat in my office looking over my patient's dental records. Looks like he moved here from Lafayette, LA not too long ago. I couldn't have known him. The things he said made me feel like he was familiar with me.

I decided to grab a bottle of water and chill in the front office with the team, until it was time to close my patient visit out. They talked about the prior week's episode of *Bad Girls Club*. Apparently, the new episode was coming on that night or the next, I was half-listening so I was unsure.

"Dr. Poirier, Mr. Green is ready for his consult. His mold is prepared for his ice grill. Also, his cleaning was one of the best ones I've had in a long time," my hygienist informed me.

"Thank you, Aniya," I smiled warmly and headed toward the exam room.

Knock. Knock. I entered after a short walk down the hallway.

"So Doc, what it's looking like? Am I'm gone be able to get my grill or what? I been wanting this shit for a long time my nigga, you feel me!" the young man spoke to me like we were friends.

"First and foremost, Mr. Green, my name is Dr. Poirier and I would appreciate it if you would refrain from using "nigga" in my office." Shaking my head at the young black man that sat before me, I was appalled by his behavior. He reminded me a Jacques back in the day.

"Cool out, Dr. P. I'm just a young nig— man tryna get by, ya heard me. Wait— I can call you Dr. P, right? Or will that put your panties in a bunch too?" he smirked, and I didn't appreciate the mockery. "Aight, I'mma stop fucking around, man. How long before I come back for my grill?" Faith asked.

Sliding my stool over to the desk phone, I hit the intercom button. "Mrs. Rose do you have a date for Mr. Green to return?" Releasing the silver button, I waited for her to respond.

"Yes, Dr. Poirier. The appointment has been set for January 26 at 2:45 p.m.," Mrs. Rose spoke through the speaker.

"Thank you," I responded and ended the conference. "It'll be ready in six weeks, just stop by the front desk and make your payment. Grill services require a fifty percent down payment to start the mold. We only accept credit or debit cards, no cash payments," I finished up the consult and shook my patient's hand.

"Fasho, Dr. P. I'mma see you next month," Faith concluded as he walked toward the door to make his exit. He stopped short and turned towards me. "Oh yeah, tell Kez and Fatts I said what's up!" with the door closing behind him, I had no chance to question his knowledge of my friends.

Walking toward my office, I noticed my door was ajar. *I know good and well this damn door was closed when I walked out of my office.* I thought, as I hesitatingly entered the room. I turned the corner behind the door and was relieved to see Kez sitting there with his head all in his phone. I didn't want my employees to meet Jap.

"What up, bro?" I asked as we slapped hands. "When did you get out of the hospital?"

"They let me out around nine this morning, my nigga," he seemed happy to be home. "Bruh, when I say I felt like I was in jail in that bitch, I ain't lying my nigga. Mr. Anderson here's your food. Mr. Anderson take your meds. Mr. Anderson don't get out of bed, you're a fall risk. Blah, blah, fuckin' blah. That shit was driving me nuts, round!" my brother had been obviously agitated his whole hospital stay.

"Bro, you was in that bih for one damn day," we laughed at my admission. "I smell food, bruh," I spoke through the laughter and hunger pangs of my stomach. Looking around I didn't see a bag. My nose was playing tricks on me.

Pulling out a brown bag from the chair next him and placing it on my desk, Kez surprised me with a shrimp salad from

Mandina's Restaurant in Mid-City. We sat and ate in silence. I was surprised to see him eating the grilled chicken with potatoes and veggies.

Breaking the silence of the aftermath of our lunch, Kez spoke up. "That lil' nigga that was leaving out when I came in looked familiar. He smiled at me. Now that I mention it, it wasn't a friendly smile."

"He was fitted for a grill, he said to tell you and Fatts what's up. I didn't know y'all had crossed paths. I wonder why he didn't just tell you himself. Where you know him from, bro?" Now more confused than ever, I asked Kez to make light of the situation.

"I don't know that nigga. Like I said, I seen him before, but I can't recall where at the moment. What's his name?" Kez questioned.

"Bruh, really? Patient confidentiality, I can't tell you his name," I responded.

"Bitch, didn't you just tell me he told you to tell me what's up? Who the fuck is the nigga?"

"His name is Faith Green and he's from Laffy. That's all I got for ya bro, I don't know him either." Violating my oath, I gave him more information than allowed.

"Nah bruh, I don't know that nigga."

Following Kez's statement, we both went into deep thought.

Chapter 7 – Zyyah

"It's been almost a month I guess. Yes, three weeks today since that little incident between Kez and I. I totally embarrassed myself by showing up to the hospital to check on the jerk." Deja laughed at me. "It isn't funny, De. It's been weeks and I still feel the sting of rejection," I complained during the habitual a.m. conversation between my best friend and me.

"I'm surprised you're off today," Deja finally stopped laughing long enough to get a response in. "Bestie, I just keep picturing the face you made when he told you he didn't remember you. I bet it was priceless," she continued to laugh, and I hung up the phone on her.

Vibrating in my hand, I hit the red button on my phone screen to ignore my best friend for the second time, since disconnecting our call. Walking into the kitchen, I decided to make breakfast before I headed out to get my hair and nails done. Working two jobs was weighing on me. I had to take today off from the restaurant.

I was only twenty-seven years old and I just wanted to be successful in my own business by thirty. When I moved to the South from the Midwest, a little under a year ago, I figured the market would be great enough to start my own bottle service. I mean, it was New Orleans, no last call for alcohol and no open container law. I should've been overwhelmed with parties, it should've been a cakewalk. When I first moved here, I did well.

Until this female named Chyna swooped in and took over the game. She was an event planner that hired her own bartenders, leaving no need for bottle service.

She was so good at her job and her passion, I followed her Instagram page. She was a sister and was beautiful so I couldn't hate or throw shade.

I flipped the television on to catch the oldest recording of Grey's Anatomy because I hadn't had a chance to watch it. I had an hour and a half before I had to leave, enough time to get in my feelings and be over it by time I made it to the shop. My eyes would have cleared up from the puffiness of having cried over the absolute saddest episode in history.

$$$$

I entered Blac-N-Keedie's, my favorite one stop beauty shop. Inside, they did hair, nails, make-up, and they had authentic, brand name purses and designer pieces in a boutique in the back. The décor in the shop was amazing. I don't know how they pulled it off, but they did. Everything in the shop was purple and red. Their mom, Des, was an interior decorator and she had a niche for things like that. She bought and designed the shop as a gift to them when she made her debut in the book world.

"Hey Zy, what's up boo?" Keedie greeted me with air kisses upon me walking into the shop. "You can sit in Blac's chair, she will be done with her client's make-up shortly." She always looked cute. She wore a red and black cheetah print plastic apron because she was coloring someone's hair. She had on gold Louboutin heels, a pair of black high-waisted pants, and a red and gold shirt that matched her shoes. She was built like a model, body just banging to the gods.

There was a little small talk in the front waiting area and I wasn't feeling it. Deciding to head to the quiet room, I found a seat and pulled out my Kindle. I started on a book titled *Caught Up Loving the Plug* by one of my favorite authors, Mesha Mesh.

As I read and snickered about November, Kenecia's wild sister, Blac interrupted my reading from the doorway. "Hey Zy, what's up boo? You can c'mon," she said, sounding like her younger sister, Keedie.

"I'm excited for this new look you have planned for me," I smiled, and we air kissed. I loved the duo that owned the shop, they were two sweethearts. Word on the street is they came from very humble beginnings; their mom was fourteen when Blac was born and fifteen months later, Keedie was born. You couldn't tell with how they treated everyone, that they were products from the environment, not of their environment. Although they were very successful, young, black business owners, they respected people from all walks of life.

"So y'all heard some new kid on the block beat Jacques down in the bathroom at Che-Che's during a one-on-one," the light-skinned woman who wasn't in the building when I arrived, gossiped.

"Girl no, not the same nigga who embarrassed my old man in front of everybody at Gabby's last year, Jacques!" The woman in the pink and green *Abercrombie and Fitch* sweat suit replied.

"Yep, girl. They said the boy made a mistake and bumped into Jacques and he lost it. He invited the boy to fight in the bathroom and got his ass kicked. Supposedly the lil' boy took his jewelry too, girl," the first woman reported like she was a newscaster.

"Un, Un," Blac mumbled behind me.

In the time that I'd been a client at this shop, I had noticed that the owners didn't engage in other people's problems. They believed that everyone had problems and no one sin was greater than the other. With that being said, they didn't judge people nor did they engage in hearsay.

"Ok, ok ladies, y'all know we don't do all that extra gossiping in here. Besides, I like Kez and we not gone drag for him in this shop, today or tomorrow."

Keedie put a stop to the gossip but answered my silent question. Yes, they were talking about *Kez*, but they got the story all wrong.

"I forgot we was in the sanctuary," the jumpsuit lady stated and laughed, then tried to hi-five the girl who started the gossip.

"No ma'am, I ain't in that. I been coming here for some years and I have preferred customer privileges. Un, un boo," the gossiper shut her down.

"I'll tell you what, Raheema, you can just go ahead and go. All my sister asked was that you cut the gossiping out. You wanna act like it was too much. Can you read bitch? There are several signs that ask that you refrain from gossip in *our* establishment," Blac pointed from herself to her sister.

Abercrombie and Fitch, now known as Raheema, grabbed her things and headed towards the door. Once she made it to the pay station, she slapped their business cards and flyers from the top of the glass case, that held products that they sold, onto the floor.

"Bitch, you done lost your mind!" Blac yelled and charged toward the front, which caused the troublemaker to exit abruptly.

"I knew you wasn't gonna catch her scary-cat ass, that's why I didn't bother," Keedie revealed, which caused us all to laugh.

The aftermath of the drama had died down. We laughed and talked until we were all done. The other ladies were very entertaining.

During the time I was there I saw pictures of people's kids, learned about marriages, relationships, and what they called relationshit. I guess relationshit is what you deal with when the relationship wasn't perfect. Show me one that was perfect and I will show you a million dollars.

The funny thing about gossip was that if you just kept your mouth shut, you could learn a lot.

$$$$

I finally decided to return Deja's missed calls. "It's my first night back at the club and I truly hope I don't have to save another ungrateful ninja," I spoke into the speaker of my phone. It sat on the dashboard as I drove to work.

"I'm not saying shit about it. You hung up on me and didn't answer when I tried to call you back. I don't wanna hear about this guy," De was persistent in not hearing about Kez. I knew how to get her to listen because she loved good tea.

"Ok, I guess you don't want the chisme that I obtained by listening to complete strangers at the shop today," I said hoping that she would've wanted to hear about what I had heard. Dead silence. "I'm gonna send you a pic of my hair, we colored it and you're gonna flip out!" I yelled, excitedly.

"Omg! Best, what did you do to your hair?" De spat out with sarcasm. I understood because I typically would take a half inch off or go from straight to curly, the simple stuff. I switched the voice call to a video chat because I didn't have time to deal with her antics. Plus, I wanted to see her facial expression when she saw the drastic change. "Aggggh, Bestie, you went purple!" Deja screamed into the video.

$$$$

"OMG, Mes'sika, will you please cover that table for me?" I asked my co-worker. Just as I was about to make my round to check on my V.I.P customers, I noticed *him*. She knew that my section always racked up nice tips and had no problems taking my tables.

> *I looked back on all those good times,*
> *We once shared, and I must've been blind,*
> *Just to think I'd find someone new,*
> *One who'd love me, better than you.*

Anita Baker crooned over the beat of the remixed background music. New Orleans had a way of dubbing Rhythm and Blues songs over upbeat music and referred to it as *That Beat*. I had done well at avoiding Kez for the night. As I closed out my register and counted my tips, we locked eyes and he smirked at me. I pretended to be so caught up in what I was doing that I looked through him. Sometimes you look in the direction of a person, but didn't see them because you're technically not looking at them. That definitely wasn't the case, but I pretended that it was. *God, he is even sexier than I remembered.*

The club shut down and the club goers had cleared out.

"Good night everyone, see you guys next week." I walked out of the back door and headed to my car. Just as I hit the unlock button on my key fob, I heard someone call my name and turned to see who it was. I didn't recognize the shadow that stood near the black Hummer truck.

I cautiously placed my purse inside of my car and stood there. I had my finger hovering over the panic button, just in case I was in grave danger. The stranger stepped out into the light and I immediately shook my head.

Chapter 8 - Jacques

"What are you doing at my job? Should I be afraid?" Zyyah fired one question after another.

"Baby girl, you need to chillax for real, for real. A nigga ain't here to hurt yo' ass." I had to get her to calm the fuck down because she was trippin'. I walked towards her and she met me halfway with her arms folded and her lip poked out. "I talked to the fellas after I got outta da hos'pila and they shed light on the lil' situation that happened here the day I got the concussion. After they left, all I could think about was how I talked to you that day you came to check on a nigga, ya heard me."

I eyed her intently. "I wanna apologize to you for acting a ass because all you tried to do was help me. I treated you like shit for coming up there because, at the time, everything was unclear. On top of me being out of it and full of them drugs they kept me pumped up with, I was skeptical of you being the enemy," Zyyah just looked at me confused.

"Why are you here now? It's been almost a month," she finally responded.

"Look, I had to get my shit together, I was in a bad way. But that's neither here nor there, I waited out chere almost two hours for you *today*, ya heard me. Come ride with me so I can make it up to you. What do you have to lose? Who knows, you might like it!" I winked at her and bit the right side of my bottom lip.

She put her hand against her mouth, placing her pointer finger over her lips. Her thumb was on her cheek. I never seen a chick do that before, I thought she was thinking about if she was gone give that snapper up or not. Says who my nigga, I was all wrong.

"Oh no you did not!" She spoke through her fingers. "I can't believe you!" she opened her hand to a hi-five and closed it to a fist with almost every word she said. Baby was a lil firecracker. "First, you did all that flirting with me. Next, I helped you and your friends. Then, you were not only rude but, you swore at me. You walk up with this piss-poor apology. Thinking I'm just gonna ride off in the moonlight with you and all would be forgiven? The nerve of you, you jerk!" She stopped for dramatic effect and held her fist next to her face. "Did you really think that I was desperate enough to fall into your bed because you gave me a weak freaking apology? You're a pig and your friends are rude and disrespectful. Tuh!" I had held in my laugh long enough.

"Ha. Ha. Haaaa," I was Bernie Mac on *Def Comedy Jam* laughing. Don't get me wrong, baby was nice. It was that the way she rolled her neck and how she sounded that didn't match, so that shit was funny as fuck. "Wit'cho white sounding ass," I was barely able to get those four words out between laughs. I was still cracking up, she did not sound like she looked. That shit had me breathless with side cramps.

"You know what, uh-uh! Has anyone ever told you that you were rude?" she questioned with an ugly scowl on her beautiful face. I was still weak, laughing. She stormed off, into the direction of her car.

"Wait, wait, wait!" I took a few steps with my long legs and grabbed her arm. She looked down at my hand like it was the plague. I threw my hands up in surrender, "My bad! Ya heard me, lil baby. I know this is no excuse, but I suck at apologizing. It's almost four in the morning so obviously you assumed I wanted to take you to the Double Tree on some sex shit. It ain't like that, baby." I knew it was time I had stopped laughing. "For real boo, let me take you out to get some breakfast. That's all I want to do," I informed her. I didn't need baby thinking I was trying to fuck, even though it was bound to happen.

A bit hesitant, she responded. "I am a little hungry. I was gonna head to Anita's anyway, I don't see anything wrong with eating together... I guess," she replied after eyeing me with careful consideration. "Before we head there, I need you to hear me out," she stared and waited for a response.

"I'm not a child so don't set no damn rules. Go head tho, ya heard me!"

"Tuh. I don't know who you think you are dealing with, or who you're used to dealing with, but I'm from a very different breed. They're Porterhouse, I'm American Wagyu. The second you are too much for me, I'm moving tables or taking my food to go. I was headed there anyway, therefore, this is not a date. Don't attempt to pay my bill. And three, I'm no one's slut, pop off, or piece of ass. Don't think you are gonna hit this because you're setting yourself up for failure," she defiantly listed her demands.

I sucked my grill, "First of all, it's jump-off not pop off, ya heard me. Get ya purse and lock your car up, baby. A nigga hungry, bruh," I responded letting her know who I was off the bat. In the words of the late rapper Soulja Slim, *either you love me, or you love me not, I'mma be me.* "The streets raised me, I'mma try to follow ya lil' demands though, ya heard me, baby," I said and meant every word.

"I'll never leave my car parked at this place, and to be frank, I don't trust you. No thanks, I'll meet you there!" She winked her eye and got into her car. I heard the motor crank. By the time I made it to my truck, she had already taken off.

If she meets me there or not, a nigga was really hungry. I had been sober since my release, I hadn't had a drink since I had been home. A nigga was on his meds and was doing well, I liked me. Don't misquote a nigga, I didn't say I was Mr. Friendly, I still busted bitches' heads off GP. After a few minutes of driving, I pulled into the always packed parking lot, hoping to find an empty spot to pull Pearl into. With all of the money they made here on weekends alone, you'd think the owners would've invested in better parking for us niggas by now.

I finally found a spot. I pulled in, hopped out, and hit the alarm. Walking into the diner, I recognized Zyyah right away. She was sitting in a back booth with her head in her phone. I headed towards her table. She finally looked up and smiled in my direction.

"I thought you wouldn't show since I didn't ride with you," she spoke softly while placing her phone into her oversized Coach bag. She was definitely different, she was label but she wasn't big name, like Michael Kors.

It was time I pulled out all tricks, because I had a feeling her ass was gonna play that hard to get shit with a nigga. I extended my arm to her and she looked at me weird.

"Let me properly introduce myself to you." She reached for my hand, damn her hands was soft as fuck. "My name is Jacques Anderson, the niggas around the way call me Kez. You can call me Bae or Daddy from this point forward," I said with a slick grin

I ain't much on Casanova,

me and Romeo ain't never been friends...

She sang out in a very melodic voice. If she kept singing like that, I was gonna have to do something to her ass up in that booth. "Keep that smooth talking over there, Mr. Charming," she smiled, and it was beautiful. "I'm Zyyah Hollins and I am not a white girl stuck in a black girl's body. In Arizona, we actually annunciate our words," she winked at me and turned her attention to the menu.

The waitress came and took our drink orders. Funny that we both already knew what we wanted, and it was the same order. Grilled chops, grits with two slices of cheese and two eggs, sunny side up still runny, with wheat toast. We sat and talked while we waited on our food.

"So, when is your birthday?" Zyyah asked.

"July 7, 1988. When is yours?" I responded.

"Thorough, are we?" she laughed. "February 10, 1987, Team Aquarius young buck," she responded causing me to stare at her. "Why are you looking at me like that, Jacques?" she asked timidly. "Hellooooo," she waved her hand in front of my face.

"My bad, lil' mama, I had zoned out. So you an Aquarius, huh? That's what's up, I know I can trust you. I ain't no psychic of the stars or nothing but word has it, Aquarius people got good hearts."

We chatted it up a bit and exchanged numbers. Zyyah was definitely a horse of a different color. I had grown to appreciate her accent in the couple of hours we had sat and talked. She was very well-spoken and intelligent. The sun was peeking through the clouds as I walked her to her whip.

$$$$

I pulled up into the DoubleTree Hotel garage and got out of my midnight blue 1970 Cutlass Supreme. Although it had been a few days since me and Zyyah had our "not date," I thought about her when I headed up to see my married bitch. Immediately, I shook that shit off because I didn't know her. Plus, a nigga wasn't in his feelings like that. I slid my keycard that I got from the front desk and walked into the room.

"Hey baby, I'm glad you showed up," my bitch purred. She had chocolate, wine, rose petals all over the bed and floor, and my favorite, a Rubenstein Bros. Bag. It was the hottest place in New Orleans to jump fresh on bitch niggas. I stayed well-dressed, and she knew I wasn't a typical nigga. I didn't shop at Dillard's or Soul Train Fashions for Polo and Girbaud. A nigga would drop a buck (one-hundred dollars) on underwear and socks only.

"What the fuck is all this shit? I know you don't miss me that much!" I questioned, confused. I spoke to her the way I did because of who she was and how she was. She was "happily" married to a rich nigga that traveled a lot. Every time he hopped on a plane, she hopped on my dick.

"Happy two-year anniversary!" she beamed with happiness.

"Damn, I been fucking the dog shit outta you for two years? Really though?" I responded while scratching my head. Damn, time had flown right pass a nigga.

"Don't say it like that, Jacques. I've given you two years of my life as you have given me two of yours. I'd think we was doing more than just fucking," she replied sadly.

"What the fuck you mean you have given me two years of your life? Say bruh, you pay to meet me at a fucking hotel, five stars might I add, once a month. We don't go nowhere, all we do is fuck. You break your weak ass husband bread with me, and we go the fuck home, ya heard me." She looked sad, but I didn't give a fuck. "All I gave your fuck ass was two years of this big dick. I don't know shit about you, your family, nothing. This ain't no damn relationship. The fuck?"

She cat crawled toward me and pulled my dick out of my pants. I knew what was about to pop off. That bitch was manipulative, but so was I. She had my dick in her hand, it was like she became one with that shit. She started beating me off and I leaned back on the bed with my elbows. She got off the bed and got down on her knees, she was bout to go in. She began to lick the length of my dick, leaving a trail of her hot saliva behind. When she got to the head, she licked the mushroom tip like it was a lollipop then swallowed it whole.

Mind you, I'm working with ten and a half, and she fuckin' swallowed me like a Percocet. She made some kind of popping sound with her lips when she pulled off of the tip that made my adrenaline rush. She was doing it in a slow motion. All of a sudden, that bitch went in like she was sucking a popsicle that was melting down her hand in the summertime. My toes started to curl and all I could do is watch my main vein disappear and reappear in her mouth.

I moaned a lil' bit because the bitch's head game was on one-hunnit. She beat me off some more and licked from the head of the dick to my balls and sucked them one by one. The most amazing part was her hand never stopped moving.

"Get in the bed bae, I don't need *him* to see rug burns on my knees," she said.

Fuck you and that nigga, I thought as I moved. I couldn't fuck the groove up. Shit, I needed some pussy. My other married bitches were on vacation and Zyyah stuck to her guns so I didn't try to fuck her.

Bitch didn't give me a chance to get settled in a spot before she was back on her knees giving a nigga that work. Her head game had my eyes rolling back in my head. It was like I was going into a deep sleep.

After she slurped that dick up like a slushy, she stood in the bed like a hood-rat and took off the lingerie that I had noticed for the first time. Next thing I know, this slut was standing over my head with her pussy leaking and started squatting down. I jumped up like it was acidic.

"What the fuck is you doing?" I growled. It was loud enough for her eyes to pop outta her head in fear.

"It's been two years, you've never went down on me. I deep-throat your anaconda and swallow your seeds with no problem," she pouted.

"Man, get the fuck on with that bullshit, bruh. I don't even kiss you, so you should know I'm not eating your married ass pussy. You fuck me once a month, no telling how many other niggas fucking once a month, too. And your husband with his outta town on business ass is fucking somebody, too. I be damn if I do anything besides fuck you, with a Magnum like I been doing," I responded.

"Kez, we ain't done here. You haven't fucked me yet and you're leaving your gifts."

I had put my pants on and made it to the door in record time.

"Bitch, we done. I don't know why I fucked your no walls having ass all this time anyway. Oh yeah," I paused. "It's because you spend all your nigga bread on me. Man, I'm out. Don't hit my fuckin line no more bruh," I stated and let the door slam behind me. All I could think about was what was in those gift bags on my way to my whip.

Chapter 9 – Chyna

It had been weeks since Naomi had her little tantrum at the restaurant. That lady had some nerves on her. She was more than a handful. I walked into the kitchen to make me some breakfast before I headed to the office. As soon as the teapot whistled, she walked in talking to someone. Realizing that the person she was talking to was with her, I tied my robe and greeted them at the opening of the foyer.

"Ah, Chyna-Sinc, what are you doing here?" she had the nerve to ask. Apparently, I had startled her.

"What the hell do you mean what am I doing here? This is my house, isn't it?" I responded quite rudely. It was like we were having a stand-off, we stared at one another waiting for someone to speak.

"Well, your car isn't here so I didn't think you were here," was her response.

"Ju'an has my car because his is… you know what, I don't owe you an explanation. I'm not understanding what my car not being here has to do with a strange man being in my home. You said you never had company over my house," I turned to the stranger. "Who are you and how many times have you visited this residence?" I waited for an answer.

"I'm not here for you. That's all that matters right, baby?" he kissed Naomi on the forehead. "You were right, she is a prude little bitch," he laughed and smacked her ass. I laughed too, and they looked at me like I was a lunatic. I walked away, and they thought they had won.

"Why did you have to talk to her like that? It was funny though, did you see her face?" I heard Naomi say behind me as the proceeded to enter my damn house.

Click. I cocked my pistol and their laughter ceased. "You get the fuck out of my house, now." I spoke to the piece of shit that accompanied my mom.

"Naomi, give me my damn key, get your shit, and get out. I'm over your disrespect," I spat fire, I was so angry, I could feel my body temperature rising.

"Disrespect? How can I disrespect you when you're my child?" She seemed utterly confused and sounded equally as stupid.

"That's where you're wrong. I'm far from the child you abandoned over twenty years ago. I'm a grown ass woman and I don't owe you shit. You walked out on me, remember? Now walk the fuck out... again. I'm done trying to mend this broken ass relationship," I was so livid, I shook. She looked like she wanted to jump on me.

"Wow, I had no idea you felt that way. You've been so giving and timid," she said.

"I have been giving, however, I've also been lenient with a lot of the bullshit you've been pulling not timid, there's a damn difference. This is it, you have taken shit too far," I pulled out my cellphone and called the locksmith on speaker. The lady was still standing there like I hadn't told her to get the fuck out of my house.

"Thank you for calling Five-Oh-Fo Lock and Key, this is James. How may I help you?" the male spoke into the phone.

"Hi James, I need a locksmith to 4772 Marigny Street as quickly as possible. I'm going to need several locks changed," I spoke urgently.

"Was there a break in and do you rent or own the home, ma'am?" he responded with matching urgency.

"No, there wasn't a break in. However, I have given someone access to my home and I no longer want them to have access, but they won't return my key. Oh, and I'm the homeowner," I responded. "Honestly, the way things are going between us, even if they returned the key, who's to say that they hadn't duplicated it?" I spoke into the speaker and cut my eyes at Naomi, who stared at me in disbelief.

"How many doors in total, ma'am?" James responded, unable to feel the tension between Naomi and me.

"I have two wrought iron screened doors that have deadbolts, and key entry doorknobs that accompany the wooden doors. Also, a single side-entry door that has both a keyed doorknob and a deadbolt. So five deadbolts and five keyed doorknobs," I spoke.

"Chyna-Sinc, are you serious right now?" Naomi finally found words to speak. "I don't even have a key to the door that is off of the kitchen, there is no need to get that changed. Actually, there's no need to get any of the locks changed, here is your stinking ass keys," she took her car key off of the ring and stared at me.

"Drastic times calls for drastic measures," I mouthed to her with a smirk.

I rolled my eyes so hard I thought I had popped a vessel. "How soon can someone get here?" I asked James. Naomi walked toward the guest room where she had been held up since she sashayed back into my life. *Freeloading ass.* I thought, and rolled my eyes again.

She came back with several luggage just as I finished up the call. She looked at me as if she wanted me to beg her to stay. Tuh, she must've lost her marbles. Here I thought she was a real one, but she got me. I was usually a great judge of character. I felt so stupid because I missed all the signs. Naomi walked past me, looking like she wanted to square up. Honestly, I was ready for her. Instead, she threw the key at me and it hit me in the center of my chest. I picked the key up from the floor and followed her down the short hallway that led to the door. Just as she put her hand on the doorknob to exit, I flung the key in her direction and it smacked her in the back of the head.

She turned to face me with an inferno burning in her eyes and I matched her glare. "Bitch!" she spat just as hot as her stare.

"Maybe, but I'm a bitch that owns shit. What are you? Do you have somewhere to sleep tonight, because I'm gonna rest well on my queen Posturepedic. I hope that broke coke head is waiting on you and he has a few dollars for a motel or maybe his own place. By the time you start the car up that I paid cash for you to drive around and do nothing in, the credit card that I loaned you will be canceled. Now, that is the true definition of a bitch, don't ya think, Sha?" I said to her with an evil smirk on my face. She spat towards me but I side stepped it and she missed. I knew she was going to try something slick, so I was prepared.

$$$$

"My facility will accommodate up to fifteen hundred guests, is that not a large enough space?" I spoke into my earpiece as I searched around my desk brainlessly. I had forgotten what I was looking for.

"I'm not sure who all will be in attendance, but I'm sure there will be plenty of space. This is more for my fiancée. I'm not a big deal in this town," the male caller spoke.

"Tuh! What do you mean you're not a big deal, Reid? You're only Reid Brignac, one of the greatest major league baseball players that has ever graced the Major League roster. You are a Louisiana native. This is a major deal," I almost yelled into the speaker. Hell, I was excited to finally see my business booming. I had booked twelve parties over the next four months, I was going to be busy.

"Thank you, Chyna, flattery gets you everywhere. Keep 'em coming!" he laughed heartily. "Email the contract to us so we can look over it. I will have Lauren send you the guestlist, menu, and her vision for the décor when we are done," Reid stated.

"No problem, hope to hear from you soon. Have a great rest of your day," I replied before disconnecting the line. I exited my office and nearly plowed into one of my senior decorators and good friend.

"Hey Casey, how's it coming along?" I asked, in reference to the décor for the biggest party I had planned in my lifetime, Ju'an's birthday party.

Never missing a step, she turned and faced me as she walked backwards. "Take a look for yourself. We are almost done with what we can do before Saturday morning. I know we have another week, but with the parties this weekend at the Marriott and the Convention Center, I'm not taking any chances," she smiled a dimpled smile and winked in my direction. I loved that she was always driven and on a mission. With her, motion was progress. She was always moving and progressing towards the finish line.

Floored by what I saw, I gave the crew the rest of the day off. I told Casey that I wanted her to take some petty cash and treat them all to an early dinner. With that, I headed out to my doctor's appointment. I hadn't been feeling well over the past few weeks, so I decided to find out what was going on with me.

Listening to the radio on the way, one of my favorite songs came on and Tamia crooned through the speakers. Whoever's idea it was to pair her with Eric Benet to create *Spend*

My Life with You, was genius. Before long, I was pulling into Dr. Farrell's parking lot. He had been my doctor since I lost my virginity to that no-good bastard, Fabian. Even the afterthought of his unworthiness made me queasy. Thank God for looking out for me and blessing me with a handsome, fun, loving man with goals and aspirations.

I wrapped my scarf around my neck and exited my car. December was usually one of the warmer months, but it had been bone-chillingly cold. Once I made it inside of the building, I pulled my gloves off and removed my large framed shades, aka hater blockers, from my face. While walking up to the sign-in desk, I noticed my favorite medical personnel and immediately smiled.

"Hey Christina, how are you today, Sha?" I queried.

"Hey Chyna, I am well. It's good to see you, you're looking great!" she returned.

"As are you, how is Cayden suge, with his handsome self?" I asked about her little one. He was so cute.

"He is bad as all outdoors, but healthy, so I'm happy," she stated with a smile. She always beamed when she spoke of her son, and that made me want a family, just for that feeling alone. We finished our chat and I sat in the waiting area. It was usually a pretty long wait, so I pulled my Kindle from my purse and picked up on Deshon Dreamz' *Stoned* where I left off. I was introduced to her writing a while back, and she could tell some stories. She was my new favorite author.

I was so into the story that I didn't hear my name being called. Raheem was bae. If he was real, I think he'd give Ju'an a run for his money.

"Chyna!" I heard Christina call my name. I looked up after bookmarking my page. I imagined I was the taste of serenity left on RJ's lips. I had to squeeze my thighs together before standing to my feet.

"What were you reading, you look flushed?" Christina asked as I approached the awaiting opened door. "Danielle called your name three times. She's new, so she isn't familiar with you. She handed me the chart as a no response. I knew you wouldn't have walked out without saying anything, which is why I got up to pull you back," she looked at me quizzically.

"Girl, Deshon Dreamz can write her ass off. I'm barely into the third chapter and now I'm ready to spend every dime on whatever she drops. You should check her out. I know you don't read, but it's a great pastime. It's almost Christmas, I may surprise you with her first series to break you in," I winked at her and brushed past her to the scale.

Removing my shoes, I held my breath. I knew I had been eating an awful lot and was not looking forward to that part of the visit. *103.3 kilograms is not ideal, but I'll take that,* I thought as the digital scale beeped, alerting us that the numbers were stabilized. After getting off of the scale, I informed Stina of my full bladder. She told me which room and that I knew the routine for urine collection, which she had been right. She worked here for as long as I had been a patient. After placing my urine in the collection container box, I headed to room six.

No sooner than I sat on the exam table and pulled my Kindle out, Dr. Farrell knocked, walked in, and shook my hand. "How have you been, Chyna?" he asked with a grey-eyed, dimpled smile.

"I've been well, Doc, thanks for asking. I'm here outside of my yearly, obviously something is going on with me. Judging by the twinkle in your eye, you have news already. Give it to me straight," I curiously summoned for answers and held my breath.

"Slow down, Chyna, I will give you what you came for. You know that I'm a bad news person first, so, here it is. Bad news is, you have gained thirteen pounds since the last visit, and I know that you have been doing well at keeping your weight down," he still looked happy, although he knew the struggle that I've faced over the years with obesity. "However, the good news is, the weight gain is onset by your pregnancy. Congratulations, Chyna. From what you've told us on your visit form, you are roughly seven weeks along. However, I want to do a full exam. After your pelvic exam, I'll have you to wait here to have an ultrasound to be positive of how far along you are," he smiled as I laid back.

Me? Pregnant? Can't be! I thought as I placed my feet in the stirrups and slid my butt to the edge of the exam table...

Chapter 10 – Jacques

"Say bruh, my married bitch is losing her fuckin mind. I cut her ass off like two weeks ago, and she been sending message after message and blowing up my line," I spoke into my Bluetooth as I drove into the direction of one of my traps.

"Bro, what's going on? Why did you cut her off? Y'all been kicking in it for a minute, huh?" Jap questioned.

"Yeah, a hot fuckin minute apparently. According to the lil' celebration she had planned for me the night I met up with her, I been fuckin her for longer than I remembered. Talm bout happy two-year anniversary and shit," I spat.

"That's some wild shit, man. You sure you ain't in love, bro? You been with her for a long time. Hell, that's longer than any relationship that I know of yours. Ha, ha," Jap joked, but I didn't find shit funny.

"Say bruh, you got me more fucked up than that bitch. A nigga ain't been with her, I been fucking her and she been breaking bread. Talm bout she been swallowing my seed all this time, and I never ate her out. Bitch, we never even ate out. Why would I? You ain't my damn woman," I got mad all over again. "That bitch lay in the bed with her husband and whoever else, the fuck I look like?" I asked rhetorically.

"Ha. Ha," Jap was still laughing as I pulled up to the house with Fatts and Kink waiting in the driveway, looking pitiful. "Bro, they just hit my intercom. My three o'clock is here. I'mma hit you later, my dude," he informed me.

"Perfect timing, my nigga. I was about to say I needed to put a fire out anyway, ya heard me!" I responded. I hopped out of my hooptie and headed towards the porch where my guys were standing. "What's up my niggas, what it's hittin' fa?" I asked as soon as I was within earshot of my lil' soldiers.

"Look, Big Foolie, I'mma give it to you straight. For starters, this spot didn't get hit, the one in The Goose did. We called you over here because it was a horrible sight at Lil' June's spot." Lil' June took over Mooney's trap last year, after he was found floating in the Industrial Canal. I was like Big Worm from *Friday.* Playing with my money was like playing with my emotions.

"What the fuck y'all niggas doing, playing games?" I questioned.

"Nah, man. The scene at the other spot is horrific. Lil' June, man, they fucked over him and everybody in the house. Even the nigga who set the whole robbery up. The fucked up part is, they had to use a silencer because nobody heard shit," Kink added to the little info that Fatts gave.

"The fuck you mean set the robbery up?" I questioned. "What makes you think they had a silencer, my nigga?" I was leery. I knew these niggas was loyal, but all of my people knew I had trust issues.

"Well, this is why we know it was a fuckin inside job. We got this note off of Dre's bitch ass. He better be fuckin glad he dead cuz I'd kill his ass if he wasn't," Fatts said and handed me a note. "And we know they had silencers because everybody in the house had to be dead for at least two days and nobody called the pigs."

"They way you kicked his ass in the chest, if that nigga wouldn't have been dead he would've died," Kink added.

Whadup old head, is day 31 n dis lil' nigga sold u out 4 10 stacks. I got dat lil' change back alone wit da stash u had in da safe. I sho do preciate it my nigga. If u open his mout, u a see dat I cut his tung out 4 being a sail out. I gotta say ur lil' dude, June, took his beat in like a man. I put 1 in his dome, den took his head off, u had a loyal 1. Fuck u n dat nigga. Lemme catch u slip'n agen like u was at da club n u next. Bitch, since u dank issa fuckin joke ol man, I'mma sho ya. Dis my final warn in, dem two black ass niggas is nex. N if I gotta take da docta out, he gone 2. Wut kinda nigga wanna be a dennis n e way. I'mma grant u a x-ten-chen, since I took out 6 niggas wit 1 2 da dome each, you got 15 days. Where I'm from, dey call me da can man cuz n e body can get it n erbody dats wit em.

"Man, this nigga illiterate as a muthafucka. I prolly can't talk worth shit, but at least I can spell, ya heard me. This shit gave me a headache, it was like solving Chinese arithmetic. Real shit tho, we need to find out who this fuck ass nigga is. He got stubs on all of us," I said to Fatts and Kink.

"That's the fucked-up part, Big Foolie. That nigga know us. We have no fuckin' clue what he look like, ya dig. How the fuck he know Jap? He been out the game," Fatts questioned like I had the answers. We all stood there in deep thought.

"Man, this nigga gotta die tonight, ya heard me. He can't breathe another day on this earth," I said to my lil' homies. "We gotta get the rest of the team and let them know to be on alert cuz this nigga is on top of his shit. He definitely did his fuckin' homework on our asses. Man, I thought all the snakes was gone. I can't believe that lil' nigga blew the fuckin' whistle on us for ten stacks. He prolly had that in his pocket with his stuntin' ass," I broke the silence.

"First things first," I pulled my lighter from my pocket, "we got to burn this shit. Anybody who attempts to read this will lose points on they fuckin IQ. This nigga gotta be the dumbest muthafucka I ever crossed paths with, ya heard me?" we all laughed as I set fire to the note. Honestly, the shit was pathetic.

"How we gone deliver the news to June's T. Jones? He was a cool as lil kid man." Kink said in reference to telling June's mama. I didn't understand Dallas slang, how they got 'T. Jones' for mama was beside me.

"My nigga, I was just asking myself how I was gone deliver the news to all they mamas," I replied with a shake of my head.

Just as we dapped each other up to leave, a lil' nigga drove by in an old school Buick Regal. It sat nice on Trues and Vogues. "Man that lil' nigga look familiar. Either one of y'all know him?" I asked.

"Nah!" they said in unison.

"Humph, see y'all at the party tomorrow, lil' ones."

With that, we all got in our cars and went our separate ways.

$$$$

Once I made it to the crib, I sat down and watched the latest episode of *Grey's Anatomy*. Miranda Bailey was bae, ya heard me. I felt my eyes getting heavy halfway through the show. Not too long after, I had succumbed to my sleepiness.

"I'm sorry, Pita. I never meant to shoot you, baby girl. You gotta believe a nigga, man. I don't hurt kids," I said to the lil' girl with two pig tails wearing an Easter dress.

"It's ok, Jacques. I know you didn't mean to kill me. I'm fine, I live with God now. I have beaucoup baby dolls and a lot of shoes. I love shoes," she said and never looked at me. She was busy sitting at her table having a tea party.

"I was sent to you to take care of you. I'm your guardian angel," Pita replied with an angelic smile, finally looking at me.

"What do you mean, Pita? You're five years old and you're dead, remember?" I probed.

She walked towards me and it was like she had a spotlight being shone on her the whole time. "I know I'm dead, silly. How else would I be your guardian angel? Duh." she questioned.

"You sure do have a smot-mouf, lil' girl. I thought we were cool?" We both laughed. She laughed so hard, she covered her face with her hands. It was like she grew mentally, but had been trapped in the five-year-old body that she died in. When she pulled her hands down, blood poured from the bullet-hole in her forehead. The blood rushed out so fast that it covered her face.

"No Pita, you can't die again. I thought you were my angel. What the hell is going on?" I questioned confused. Was God punishing me?

"I'm not dying, silly goose," she responded and wiped the blood from her face. When she wiped the blood from her face, it had been transformed into the face of the dude from the car...

I shook myself awake and grabbed my heat. I was sweaty as a muthafucka. I looked around while I huffed and puffed, like I had just run a race.

"What the fuck? It was the nigga Faith. The nigga in Jap's office is the nigga that busted me in my head and killed my family."

He just didn't know his fucking days were numbered.

Chapter 11 – Jap

Of all half-days, it was the only Saturday that I didn't want to work. Not that I was a lazy bum or anything, it was my birthday party and I had been anticipating it. It was supposed to be a surprise, but I overheard Chy telling Casey about the color scheme and had been excited ever since. Sadly, Chy had to also get Casey to find a caterer. Being that she had lost her partner and best friend, Ghladis, who had been taking care of that aspect of the company since they started out of Chy's living room, she had no choice.

"Well, it's been a great day today, ladies and gent. Will I see any or all of you at the party tonight?" I asked my team. We hired a new kid, a guy named Earl. He was a dental assistant who showed interest in furthering his career as a dentist. I gladly accepted his application. It was hard to influence young black men. He came in hungry for success, so that was a win. Hopefully one less kid we loss to police brutality or worse, black on black crime.

"We have been talking about this party for months. We're all gonna be there, Dr. P," Tarsha admitted and everyone looked at her.

"Only one rule for tonight, and that is to call me Ju'an," I said as I registered what she had said. "Wait, what do you mean months? I just gave y'all invites two weeks ago." I recalled.

"Boy, Tarsha, you can't hold water, huh?" Aniya asked.

"I mean, it's not like I spoiled the surprise, he found out right after we did so…" Tarsha replied putting her hand out like 'duh'. "Anyways Dr. P., I'm ready to get turnt up," she finished, while doing the popular Nae-Nae dance.

"Tarsha, I don't know if I wanna see you turnt if you this wild without a drink," Big E said to her.

"Whatever young buck, you can't drink so, you can be my designated driver. Wait, you do have a license, right?" she winked at him and he smiled. Surprisingly he didn't snap back, he was usually quick on his feet with comebacks.

"Alright then y'all, I'm out. I have to get my clothes out of the cleaners, so I will see y'all later tonight. Oh, and remember, it's by invitation only. So make sure your plus one is either with you, or on the guest list."

With that, I left the office and ran a few errands before heading home.

$$$$

I pulled up to Chy's building and the parking lot was lit. I'm so glad I had a reserved parking spot. I group texted my fam to see if they had already made it because I didn't happen to see any of their whips.

Me: Aye yo where y'all niggas at bruh???
Message read: 9:54 p.m.
Fatts: Say bruh you know I'm here, a nigga is punctual
Message received: 9:55 p.m.
Kez: I'm in route, I had to wait on my +1 sexy ass. Calm down bitch a nigga gone be there (crying laughing emoji)

Message received: 10:00 p.m.

Fatts: Kink where u at cuz

Message received: 10:01 p.m.

Kink: Just found parking, I was on the phone with T.

Jones. Pops ain't doing well. But that's a convo for

another day.

Message received: 10:03 p.m.

Me: Sorry to hear that dawg.

Message sent: 10:05 p.m.

We all met up at the entrance and chatted it up for a minute before we walked in. I knew my baby was talented, but damn, she did her thing on the décor. It was themed just the way my alter-ego Jap, would've liked it. Most parties in December were Christmas-themed, with the red, green, and gold colors. Not this one, though. Chyna and Casey hooked me up with my favorite colors. Everything was blue, black, and a hint of silver, including the photo booth background. Walking up to the bar, we all ordered our usual drink. For me and Fatts, who by the way was underage, it was V.S.O.P brandy straight. I was surprised to hear Kez order a Coke on the rocks.

"Say cousin, you drinkin' or nah?" Fatts said to Kink. I knew he was thinking about his pops. Hell, if it was me, I would've been on that state, headed to Dallas.

"Nigga, does a bear wipe his ass with a white rabbit, in the woods, after he take a shit? Hell yeah! It's a celebration, ain't it, cuz?" With that, he gave us a half grin and ordered the whole bottle of Ace of Spades Champagne. "Nigga, you brought your girl up in here. True, we met her in passing, but you could at least formally introduce her, damn," Kink said after turning his bottle up.

"Zyyah, everybody. Everybody, Zyyah," Kez responded. "Say bruh, I'mma need you to stop eyeballing my date, my nigga. You been on her since the night at the club," he said to Kink.

"Psst nigga, I thought you couldn't remember shit?" Kink responded with a laugh.

"I can't, but I remember that, bitch. Ha. Ha. Haaaa," Kez laughed. Because I had known him most of my life, I knew the laugh was a cover up. He was dead ass serious.

"Oh my God, like, really Jacques?" Zyyah said in a very articulate tone.

"Where are you from, Zyyah?" I asked and looked at Kez. "Calm down killer, I have mine. Don't give me the death eyes." We all laughed. At that moment the ice had been broken. That dude had serious trust issues, which is why it's surprising to see a female on his arm at my party tonight.

"Born and raised in Phoenix, AZ. Ever been?" Zyyah informed and asked me.

"Nah, I haven't been anywhere west of Dallas. Let me introduce you to my ol' lady," I said to her. "It's aiight if I take her to meet Chy, huh bro?" I chuckled.

"What's so funny punk ass, fuck you laughing fa? Do you mind if I do the honors, bitch? I mean, she is my date and Chyna is my sister," Kez countered back.

"I know this is a shake of a duck's tail in the wind, but I'll ask anyway. Is your girlfriend, Chyna of Chynamic parties?" Zyyah asked and reminded me of an old soul.

"You know my baby?" I asked. I felt a burst of pride rush through my veins.

"Well, technically, I don't know her. I follow her Instagram page. Her gift is a blessing from God. Her work is amazing," Zyyah smiled genuinely. Her eyes lit up and it made me feel like bae was celebrity status.

"Let me take you to meet her, boo," Kez stated and broke the bond that was being created between Zyyah and I. Hating ass nigga.

"Please do, I definitely don't want to be a fifth wheel, tagging along with you and your guy friends," Zyyah stated. Kez and I headed up to the second level with Zyyah behind me and him behind her. Straight protection mode as we did with the females of our crew. I knew we would find Chyna there, most likely in her office.

"Baby," I announced as I walked into the office. Chyna jumped and put something in her desk drawer. I blew it off as a surprise and didn't question it. "Kez has someone he wants you to meet," I informed her. She stood to her feet and tugged at her already loose-fitting shirt. *Damn my baby is sexy as fuck right now… a few more drinks and I'mma fuck her in this office.*

Kez walked in with Zyyah on his trail. He hugged Chy and her eyes lit up as she smiled at Zyyah. "Hey, I know you, don't I?" she said

"Yes, we met briefly, several weeks ago. I was you and the older lady's server at Copeland's," Zyyah told Chyna. Kez got him a humble one, I hope she wasn't after his money.

"Well it's nice to formally meet you, Sha. Please, have a seat. Y'all can go now, thank you. We'll be down soon," Chyna shooed us off like we were kids. I can't say I liked that.

We headed back downstairs. It was lit. I don't know how Chy got the guest list together, but she did great at weeding out the bad seeds. We did our gangster for a while. That nigga Kink was like a kid in the candy store. Every time I looked up he was on a different female and a new bottle of Ace. He said it was a celebration, and that nigga was lit.

$$$$

The party was everything a nigga never had. I mean, I was raised by a single father, there were no parties. All he cared about was making sure I was clean, fed, loved, and had a roof over my head. I wasn't bitter about it, I actually thanked him for being a loving and active father, rather than a nigga who worked so much I barely knew him, kind of man.

We thanked everyone for coming out and I was blessed to have had a whole party full of young black people without any infractions. I guess Kink found what he was looking for, because he had Tarsha on his arm all through the night.

After the cleaning crew came in, we all headed out. Kez and Zyyah were standing off to the side, Fatts and Toy were near them, and Kink and Tarsha were opposite us. Just as Chyna put the key in the door, Kez and I took notice of a car creeping by. As we all dapped each other up and were getting ready to go our separate ways, we heard wolf-like sounds being screamed out.

By the time we looked up, it was too late. A dude was sitting on the window opening of the passenger side facing us, howling. It was the same car that had just passed. He had a TEC-9 pointed in our direction. Shots rang out. *Tat tat tat tat tat tat tat.* "Fuck you, bouzins!(bitches)"

Urrrrrrrrrrrrrt! The tires screeched, as the unknown vehicle peeled off and left us in a cloud of smoke and a daze.

Fatts and Kez ran into the street and opened fire, we heard glass shatter, but we didn't know if the target had been hit.

When the smoke cleared, and we looked around to check on everyone, it was a sight to see. I looked to my right and saw Kink. He was sitting with his back against the wall holding Tarsha in his arms. She appeared to be dead as blood poured from her mouth. I looked at Chyna, her stomach bled profusely.

"Oh my God, Chyna, you're bleeding!" Zyyah yelled. At that point, everyone freaked out.

To my left, Fatts stood cussing and yelling while Kink attempted to revive Tarsha.

"She's gone, cousin, you just exhausting yourself for nothing. Ain't no saving her, my dude," Fatts said to Kink. Kink ignored him and kept doing CPR.

I paced because I couldn't imagine life without bae. Yeah, we had a rough start, but I loved her. She had been through enough with being raped, beaten, cheated on, forced to have an abortion, and losing her best friend at the hands of her own dad. "Cut us a break, Lord. What did we do to deserve this?" I fussed at God.

"Ju'an," Chyna called out for me. I walked over to her, she reached her hand out for me. I kneeled down and held her securely as I applied pressure to her wound. I hoped the ambulance got here soon since Zyyah called. Her speech was articulate, they may have assumed she was white and sent the ambulance faster than they would have for one of us.

"Agggggggh! We gotta get the fuck outta here, my nigga! We gotta go, we gotta go!" Kez screamed. I don't know what had gotten into him, I had never seen him so freaked out at a scene of a crime.

"Big Foolie, look at me bruh, look at me. We aight bruh. Calm down and take a few breaths." Fatts and Toy had run over to him and were trying to cool his rage down.

We heard sirens in the distance. "Them folks coming, I need y'all to get rid of y'all heaters, NOW!" I guess that request snapped Kez back from wherever he had drifted off to.

"Gimme ya shit, Slim. I can't fuck around with the blue swine," Kez said to Fatts. Fatts handed his pistol to Kez. "Baby, we gotta go and I need you to drive because my nerves is too fuckin' bad," he said to Zyyah. "Jap, hit me up with the location. Love you, sis. You better hang in there. I can't deal with this shit again," he kissed Chy on the forehead, dapped me up, ran across the street, and jumped in the truck.

The police and ambulance pulled up within seconds of each other. They started with all the questions while the EMT's worked on Chy. They took a look at Tarsha and told Kink they were sorry for his loss, but she was dead on arrival.

"My nigga, can you let this man go to the hospital with his girl? I will answer all the questions you need, bruh," Fatts didn't care who he talked crazy to. I knew he was boisterous, but he was bucking on N.O.P.D., a white cop at that.

$$$$

"Ju'an Poirier?" A short white doctor with red shoulder-length hair called.

"Yes ma'am, I'm right here," I got up from my seat in the waiting area and walked over to her.

"Ms. Green has you listed as her proxy. I would like to speak to you in reference to her care. For starters, you can breathe. The wounds are superficial because the bullet went straight through the excess skin on her left side. It did take a very small piece of flesh, but it didn't affect any vital organs. She's lost a lot of blood, but she will make a full recovery," she took a breath.

"Also, you both should be ecstatic to know that the baby wasn't affected. We had to give her two units of blood, stitch her up, and now she's sedated and asleep. We will monitor both her and the unborn fetus' vital signs as a precaution. Being that she isn't that far along, we want to make sure they are fully out of the woods," she smiled at me, Kez, and Fatts, who had finally made it to the hospital. "Any questions, Mr. Poirier?"

Baby? I thought to myself as I stood there dumbfounded. I had a million questions, but at that point, I couldn't think of one.

"I have one question, but it's not for you. Riddle me this *Dr. Poirier,* you keepin secrets now? When was you gone tell us we gone be uncles?" Kez asked me.

"Bro, I'm trying to figure out when Chy was gone tell me that I was gonna be a dad!" I scratched my head.

Chapter 12 – Faith

I finally landed in the N.O. from Shreveport, Louisiana. I been causing so much ruckus, that shit was getting hot. The first week I was here, I had to bust a nigga in his shit. I was asked to come here by my dad to tie up some loose ends. I haven't seen that nigga since I got here. Hell, I saw him more when he visited us in the Port.

I'm Faith, I'm nineteen years old and I have a twin brother named Hope. We never liked our names. We were often bullied for being of mixed races, or biracial and having feminine names. That's why I had a *don't give a fuck* attitude. Momee said after dealing with our father, Pappi, and his sinister ways, she needed hope and faith in her life. That's where our punk ass names stemmed from.

Hope was the subtler one. I guess it was because he was older by four minutes, which was why he was more mature. Me, on the other hand, back home they called me the Can Man. I felt like anybody can get it and everybody that's wit em.

Bzzz! Bzzz! Bzzz! My phone vibrated alerting me of a text.

Pappi: Get ya brother and meet me at the watering hole, now yeah!

Message received: 3:37 p.m.

Me: we b dere when we get dere fuck azz nigga
**backspace, delete **

Me: Yessuh, we OTW

I was tired of him bossing me around like some sucka ass nigga. He could get what them bitch niggas on the block last night got, any day of the week. I gots zero fucks to give.

"Aye Hope, yo' bitch ass paw wanna see us," I yelled into the other room for my twin.

He came out looking nervous. "What does he want now?" he questioned like I knew or some shit.

"I don't know, nigga. He just sent me a text saying meet him at the watering hole. When you gone stop being so scary? That's the one thing that pisses me off about you!" I queried.

"When you gone stop being so fuckin' reckless? That's one of the many things that pisses me off about you. You run the fuckin streets like a wild man and I'm left being the clean-up man!" Hope was livid. I had never seen him that mad, at me anyway.

"That's all ya punk ass good for G, cleaning up!"

When I said that, it set him off. He swung on my ass and we tussled for a few minutes. We fucked each other up with body blows, pound for pound. We hadn't scrapped like that since we was about eleven or twelve. Something else was bothering him, it was much deeper than the surface.

"Man, what the fuck is wrong with you, bitch?" I asked through rugged breaths.

"You shot two fuckin' women last night, that's what's wrong with me, nigga. Them people didn't do shit. You didn't even hit the target, ol' dumb ass. You are too fuckin' reckless, man. One is dead and the other one is in the hospital." That nigga scolded me like I gave a fuck who got killed.

Maybe them niggas would get the picture and get off the streets since nobody ain't safe out ya. I thought. I was too out-of-breath to wrestle with his duck ass again.

After he glared at me with a death stare, he opened his nagging ass mouth, "I just can't with you, bruh. You've reached the age in life where you are beyond redemption and beyond help. If you don't straighten up soon, you gone find yourself by yourself," Hope said and shook his head.

"The fuck you mean I'mma find myself by myself, nigga? We came in this world together so I'll neva be alone," I responded. I knew that nigga was just talking, at least I hoped he was.

$$$$

We pulled up to the location to meet Pappi and he looked pissed. That nigga was red as a boiled crawfish. He was pacing and smoking a joint.

"Let me hit that 'white-boy', Pappi," I referenced the weed rolled in EZ Wider rolling paper, when we got within arm's reach. He looked at me with the same death stare that I often looked at my enemies with. I guess the shit was hereditary.

"What happened last night, yeah?" Pappi asked as he passed me the joint. I hit that shit and coughed for a good minute before I responded.

"I burnt up the block. You told me to get them niggas coming out the party, and that's what I did," I answered.

"No. You choot someone very near and dear to me, yeah. And killed someone else innocent child. The targets are still walking, they still da issue, coo-yon (fool)."

When I was young, I was confused at most of the shit he said. Back then, I didn't understand the Cajun language.

"How was I supposed to know you had people there? You said the enemy was there and to light them up. I don't give a damn who got shot. I don't know none of them muddafuckas."

Pappi turned three shades redder, his white skin had turned the same color of my mixed-race skin.

He slapped the fuck outta me before I could blink, and Hope's bitch ass just sat there and watched with a hoe ass smirk on his face.

My jaw was burning, I knew it had turned red.

"What da hell you hit me fa?" I was confused and pissed.

"You choot ya sister, dumb ass, and you don't give a damn. Me not feelin dat, no," he informed us.

"Sister!" me and Hope yelled in unison. I was livid. I thought we were his only kids. Why the fuck had he not been told us anything about a damn sister?

"Well, how many more siblings should I be worried about? You sent me out ya head first and got the nerve to be upset cuz I almost killed the illegitimate sister."

I realized I further pissed him off when he grabbed me around the neck and body slammed me on the hood of his Audi. That nigga was quick and strong, I never saw it coming.

"Pappi, let him go! You are gonna kill him," I heard Hope finally step up. I was losing consciousness. Sin was a big ass white man, one of his hands were as big as both of mine together.

"Pappi, you crazy as fuck, man. The first thing you should have done was warned me against the girl. You should have told me she wasn't a part of the war, anything man, fuck," I gasped for more air but never missed a beat while talking shit.

"Pappi, we have a lil' sister? How old is she? Where's she from? I want to meet her," Hope's ass-kissing ass wanted to meet the bitch that I almost killed. I didn't wanna meet the hoe, no new siblings.

"She ain't ya lil' sista, no. She's almost thirty and she was raised here wit me. Her momee put her thru some tings. I took her from Naomi and raised her by myself," Pappi learnt us.

While Hope was excited to meet her, I wanted to know what was so special about her,
that she was kept hidden.

Chapter 13 -Hope

I'm Hope, Faith's identical twin. We were the epitome of identical, same height, same weight, same taste in clothes, same eyes, same everything. The people that actually knew us, could only tell us apart by the very distinctive birthmark on Twin's right ring finger. We caused hell for people that couldn't tell us apart, especially girls.

It had been several hours since we found out that Faith and I weren't Pappi's only children. A big sister? I couldn't believe I had another sibling. Her name is Chyna-Sinc Green. Not only did we share blood, but we also share the same surname. Why Pappi kept it hidden from us wasn't a factor to me, but it seemingly bothered my twin brother, Faith.

Back in Shreveport we were raised by our mother, Janyce. Pappi would pop in and out whenever he felt the need. Although he'd stay for a few days whenever he did, he wasn't a constant. I now understood why. Nonetheless, I respected him as a man and as my dad, simply because we were raised in church and I lived by "Honor thy mother and thy father".

I was troublesome until around age fourteen. A stolen car and the possession of a gun with murder charges on it, landed me and twin in a juvenile detention center. We argued that the car had already been popped and that we found the gun inside. However, being two young black teens in that area, raised red flags. Having a praying mom and a well-to-do father was the only thing that saved us from spending our lives in prison.

Pappi found a lawyer that combed over our cases with a fine-tooth comb. She found the flaws that the pigs and the D.A. didn't. For instance, the bullets in the clip of the gun held all the evidence they needed to prosecute the right person. The same prints were found at the crime scene and also on the trunk of the car, where apparently, they had stowed the body before dumping it in the Atchafalaya Basin.

After all of that occurred, I fell to my knees and changed my ways because the good Lord had given me a second chance. Don't misquote me, I never said I was an angel. I still dabbled in the streets, but it was a rarity. I felt that at age nineteen, I wasn't where I could've been, but I wasn't where I used to be either. That was a blessing and I received it.

After the meeting with Pappi and finding out about Chyna, I was determined to meet her. I knew Twin had almost killed her, and Pappi warned me against the goons that were protecting her, but it was a risk I was willing to take. Pulling up to the hospital, I decided to sit in my car for a few minutes. I contemplated whether I should go against the grain and take the risk, or just listen to Pappi and leave it alone.

"Fuck it, she's my sister. I'm going to introduce myself to whoever I need to, to meet her," I talked myself into getting out of the car.

As I usually did during the winter months, I pulled my hoodie over my head and walked up to the entrance. Stopping at the front desk, I asked where Chyna Green was located and proceeded to the location of her room with caution.

As I exited the elevator, I noticed the dude that was staring at me the other day when I was driving down the street. I didn't know him but, his eyes gawked at me as if he had a vendetta. Deciding to sit in the waiting area playing on my phone, I remained incognito and watched as everyone came and went to Chyna's room.

A couple of dark-skinned dudes left with a beautiful melanin chick. Then the dude that wanted to kill me and a thick female left soon after. I knew there was one more. Pappi said her boyfriend's name was Sap or Jap or some shit like that, and to what little knowledge I had, he hadn't walked out. I turned my attention back to my phone, I was trying to kill my high score on *Subway Surfer*. I was so into it that I almost missed my cue.

"Ok ladies, I've been kicked out of the hospital to go take a shower. You see I'm still full of blood, but that's what love does to you, right?" a male voice laughed followed by a few giggles from the nurses.

"Ok Ju'an, we know you'll be back," one nurse insisted.

"Right, he will be back before his skin dries," a different voice agreed.

"Let that man be in love, it's what we all want. Someone to love us unconditionally. Do you, Dr. Poirier; I admire y'all's love. It makes me believe that my king is out there somewhere," a soft-spoken woman admitted. I wanted to see her, she sounded cute and like she needed me in her life.

Dr. Poirier? That nigga crazy for real, twin got this man fitting him for a grill, I thought. I couldn't imagine that Pappi wanted to take his own daughter's man from her. Then again, Momee ended up in the Psychiatric hospital for almost a year, fucking with him. That's another story, for another book.

The moment he walked past me, tucked away in the corner unnoticed, I waited for the elevator doors to close. That was when I made my move, I walked past the nurse's station and winked at the young-looking chick as her eyes twinkled. She must've been the one that was talking about her king. When I made it to my sister's door, my nerves started to get the best of me.

In through my nose, out through my mouth. In through my nose, out through my mouth, I repeated the mantra from the outside of her door, to her bedside. She was resting peacefully. I couldn't believe how much we favored. She looked like twin with hair, or twin looked like her without hair. Either way we all looked the same, just like Pappi. *I wonder if she has murky green eyes like us?* I questioned myself.

"Hi sissy, I'm your little brother, Hope. Pappi just told us we had a sister today. I'm pissed that he deprived us of the past nineteen years of getting to know each other. I'm so happy to know that we have a sister. I hope you wake up before I leave so we can talk," I paused and took in her natural beauty. "I'm gonna write my number down and put it inside of this purse over here. If you can actually hear me and happen to find it, please call me so we can link up to get familiar," I grabbed her hand and kissed it. With that, I had nothing more to say to my big sis. I turned to leave just as the door opened. *Damn, I'm busted.*

"Who are you?" the cute little nurse from the nurse's station asked.

"I'm Hope, Chyna's little brother," I smiled.

"I can tell, you guys have the same eyes," she smiled back.

Well, I guess that answered my question. With that tad bit of information, I headed home to share the news with Faith, although he pretended not to care.

Chapter 14 – Sinclair Green

I was pissed that Kez and Jap was still upright. My baby girl was laid up in a hospital bed because da chooter was reckless. Had I not been watching the news for follow up, I would have never known dat Chyna-Sinc's life was endangered. I guess dat was the result of sending a doe to do a buck's job. I never meant for me bebe to be physically harmed, emotionally and mentally, she would've eventually healed. Dat type of physical harm was gonna do a number on her. She can't ever find out it was me who sent the hit.

I decided to go to the hospital to see me bebe, to make sure she was doing well. Channel 6 news didn't say if it was life-tretnin or not, so I guess I had to go up dere and check for myself. Grabbing the keys, I locked up the dry cleaners and headed to the hospital. I knew if I had waited to see her at her home, I wouldn't have had the chance.

Pulling up, I realized it was getting late and I knew I may have had trouble once me got inside. Especially if Kez and Jap was in dere. Not so much Jap but Kez, dat boy was a live wire near a pool full of people. I walked up to the desk and asked where my daughter was located. Within a few minutes, I was at her bedside.

"Me bebe, I hope you can hear me, yeah Sha. me sorry for all da bad tings dat happen to you ova dis past year, yeah. If I could take it all back I would, Sha. I hope you pull tru dis cuz I can't go on widout cha, no," I paused and stared at me bebe, the girl I raised to be a woman all by myself. Well, with the help of my good friends Vicki and her husband. I couldn't help the fact dat it was my fault Chyna-Sinc was laid in dat bed. I felt like a son of a bitch standing there unaware of the damages done to'er.

I never meant for any of this to happen to me bebe. I'm just glad dat you ain't as cruel as I am God. I know dat Ghladis is continuing to rest in paradise and watching over me bebe from her Madison in da sky. There is no other explanation as to why she still here tonight. Thank you God and Ghi. I crossed my heart and looked to da ceiling, after dat silent conversation with the man upstairs.

"I never got to say dat I was sorry about wat happen to Ghladis. She was me bebe too, you know dat, Sha. I loved her like she was my own. I miss her crazy behind. I always look at her picture and regret evertin about dat night at da plantation. She called me to check on me as much as you did," I said, starting to tear up tinking about her. Looking at me bebe laying there peacefully, I couldn't help but tink if it was my destiny to lose my daughter for taking Vicki and Glenn's only child.

"While you are laying here, and I have da chance to explain my reasoning for gettin rid of dat bitch who called herself a muda. When you was a tot, barely two or three yas old one of me friends dat help me start da cleaners came to me wid a revelation and you in tow," I paused to contain my rage.

"He say me needed to get home and get dere fast because Naomi was tryna sell you fa drugs," I admitted to a sleeping Chyna. "I didn't wanna believe him, but I knew he ain't have no reason to lie on Naomi. He went on to tell me dat she tried to sell haself to him and he refused. When he did, she offered you ta him, Sha. Her own flesh and blood, her baby girl, for heroin? I could've killed her. Instead, I sent her off widout a second thought, me bebe. Anytin to save you from the negative wondas of da world," I said. Just the thought of the horrific day caused me blood pressure to rise.

The door opened, and I cringed. I didn't want any drama wit dese young bucks in this hospital.

"Say bruh, what are you doing here?" Jap questioned me.

"What do you mean what am I doing here? Dat's me bebe in dat bed, ain't it?" I countered back.

"She hasn't been your *bebe* in almost a year. When she was at her weakest point, you walked out on her. You need to get the fuck out of here," he responded.

"Listen you little muddafucka, I shoulda killed ya punk ass when me had da chance. I don't give a damn if da gates of hell woulda opened up and flooded da eart with spawns of Satan, none of you bouzins woulda stop me from comin see about me bebe," I said as I walked up to dat little bastard. We were nose-to-nose getting ready to tee off when we were interrupted.

"What the hell are y'all doing?" Chyna woke up and questioned. Her voice was so faint, it was barely recognizable. I knew I had messed up, bad.

"I'm about to take ya boyfriend out if he don't get his ass outta me face. Who died and told him he was the ruler of your gates?"

As soon as the phrase left my lips, I immediately regretted the word choice.

"Because I'm familiar with the look in your eyes, I'm going to forgive the verbiage you used. What are you doing here, Pappi?" Now my own daughter was questioning my presence. Jap relaxed and took his stance next to his woman, as he should have.

"I needed to see you after watching the news. We both know the news channels can blow tings outta proportion," I responded calmly. Although I wanted to snap on her for sounding like an ungrateful little princess, I couldn't. If we were being honest, I didn't belong in her room. I didn't deserve to visit me bebe after everytin' I had put her through.

"Baby, I need you to take a seat. I have a few questions I need Pappi to answer," she told Jap and he obliged, but never let her hand go. "First, I've been awake the whole time, therefore, I heard everything you said. I truly appreciate your apology about Ghi, it's all I've been waiting for. I forgive you, now, you gotta forgive yourself," she looked at me, and I could feel the sincerity of her forgiveness.

"Do you have kids outside of me?" she asked. It trew me for a loop.

"Dat was a curveball, where did dat come from, Sha?" I replied, not knowing if I should just be honest since she had wiped the slate clean.

"It's a question, I had a dream that someone came up here talking to me. He told me that he was my brother. He kept saying *we* didn't know *we* had a sister. Do you or don't you have other kids, Pappi?" she asked, demanding an answer.

I stood silent, as if time had stopped. I wanted to answer, I truly did, but how was I gonna explain to her that I had another family dat she neva knew about? She looked like a light bulb had went off in her head.

"Babe, pass me my purse, please," she asked and Jap handed her the bag that sat on the chair near the bed.

"Sooooo, you gonna answer me or stand there like the cat got ya tongue?" she questioned as she rummaged through her purse.

"Well, me bebe," I paused. Just as I was gonna say something she pulled out a tattered piece of paper and held it up for me to see.

Hope

504-758-1822

Call me big sis. (smiley face)

"It wasn't a dream at all," she stated matter-of-factly. "Who is Hope? Better yet, who is the *we* that he mentioned and how old are they?" she asked. I couldn't do notin but tell her the truth. The proof was in the pudding.

"Da cat is outta da bag, all I can do is tell you da true. Me went shrimpin abut twenty-one years ago and met a woman, yeah. We had a ting goin on. Me would see her every other week, and a year later, she got pregnant. She wanted to move here from Lafayette, but me didn't want to trust no one around ya no, Sha," I admitted a half truth and omitted the other half.

"Understood, but I still don't get how he knew to come here. Also, you still haven't said who he was referring to when he said *we*," she responded, sounding like the bossy little girl that she had always been.

"Hope and Faith are your nineteen-year-old twin brothers. They moved here not too long ago and came by my house earlier and saw your pictures on the mantle. They started askin da same questions you askin, Sha. Who, what, when, where and I told them what I saw on the news."

"So, why didn't the other one come?" she asked.

I smiled, causing her to smile, questionably. "Because Faith is bull-headed and stubborn like you, Sha. Hope is the friendly one," I learnt her. I looked over at Jap and noticed he looked a little uneasy. "Why you lookin like you saw a ghost, buck?"

"Oh, no reason. Just thinking about something, old head," he responded.

"Last question, how true is what you said about Naomi trying to sell me for drugs?" Tank God she heard dat part cuz I know Naomi only wanted one ting and dat was money.

Chapter 15 – Kez

It was a couple of days before Christmas. Me and Zyyah had been talking and texting more than hanging out. It was different for me because, I hadn't really talked to a single woman in years. I only fucked with married bitches. It was just easier for me not to get attached to a bitch that was going home to her husband. Since the shooting, she had dove head-first into working long hours on both jobs. She said she was working hard so she can get her coins up to start her own business. But honestly, I think it was to avoid me, because of all the crazy shit that popped off at Jap's party a couple of weeks ago.

With all that had happened, I wouldn't blame lil' mama for not wanting to fuck with me. What I wanted though, was for her to be honest. Honesty and loyalty was everything to me and anyone who knew me, knew that my mother had raised me that way. Even if it did fuck me up mentally, she was always truthful.

When I picked Zyyah's ass up, she was gonna have to be one hunnit with me. I had been anticipating this date for some time, I felt like a teenager all over again. When I picked her up for Jap's party, she made me wait at the office for her, saying that she lived in the middle of the complex and it was closer for her to walk rather me drive around to her building. I thought it was bullshit, but I went with it.

After I got out of the shower and got dressed, I sprayed a lil' Issey Miyake in the air and did a walkthrough. I liked to smell fresh, but not too overpowering. I got that slick move from my mother. She loved her smell goods. I grabbed my keys and headed to Green Tree Apartments. Getting there a few minutes early and knowing that women took a bit longer to ready themselves, I pulled my phone out to scroll on Instagram. I always liked to laugh at the stunted-out ass people, they would tend to forget that most of their followers knew them in real life.

As soon as I clicked to like a picture, my phone rang, and it was that crazy ass bitch that I had been avoiding. Deciding to answer, I took a deep breath and prepared myself for what the married hoe had to say. I knew I shouldn't have answered, being that I was outside waiting on my date, but curiosity got the best of me.

"Hella?" I said nonchalantly.

"Hey bae, I been missing you. Can you meet me at the spot?" Faye cooed through the earpiece.

"Bruh, you really gone call my phone and act like I hadn't been avoiding ya fuck ass?" I yelled into the phone.

"What's wrong with you, Ja-Ja?" she called me by a pet name that I hated with a passion, and she knew it.

"Bitch, didn't I tell you not to call me that? I can't deal witcha nutty ass. If you don't fall back, something gone happen to you," I growled.

"Is that a threat, Jacques Anderson?" she asked, perplexing me because I never told the bitch my last name. "Oh you didn't think I knew you, Kezzy Pooh? Get your muthafuckin' ass to the spot before I spill everything I know about you. I have photos and videos, bitch nigga! It's called a private investigator," she countered back with a threat.

"Ha, ha, ha. I knew you was a crazy ass bitch. I have photos, names, and addresses. Do you still live at 13234 Chateau Court, New Orleans, Louisiana 70129? Is your husband travel agency still located at 7731 Henley Street, New Orleans, Louisiana 70126? Does your daughter still attend Immaculate Heart of Mary with a half day on Fridays?" I laughed wickedly at her silence.

I heard a gasp and the call time was still running, so I knew she was still on the other end. Probably in a state of wonder, the fuck she thought. My money was long too, probably longer than hers because I was a greedy ass nigga.

"Hella? Your silence is so loud, it's piercing my eardrums. Don't ever fuckin threaten a real nigga, ya heard me, bitch. Call me a bitch ever aga— matter of fact call my phone ever again and I'mma start with ya fuckin kid, hoe. Lose my fuckin' number, you community pussy having slut."

"Ok, you win... for now. Tell that fat bitch to keep an eye out for me," she responded and ended the call.

Tap. Tap. Tap. I heard someone pecking on Pearl's window. That stupid ass bitch had a nigga nerves so bad, I had been thrown of my square. I didn't even notice Zyyah walk up to the truck, that could've easily been a jack-boy. Unlocking the doors, she hopped in. I wanted to be a fuckin' gentleman and open the door for her but this bitch, Faye, threw a wrench in that plan for being who my mother raised me to be.

"Hey, Jacques," she stated as she got settled and secured her seatbelt.

"How you doing, Zyyah?" I tried to hide any inkling of being pissed the hell off. It wasn't her that I was mad at and she didn't deserve to have that part of me due to somebody else pissing me the fuck off.

"I'm doing well. How are you? Judging by the frown lines, I'm not sure if we should move forward with the date or reschedule," she acknowledged my being upset. *Damn, she's observant like a muthafucka. She barely looked at me,* I thought.

"I'm glad you finally made time for a nigga," I smiled faintly, blowing off her weak attempt to reschedule.

"I'm going to allow you to blow-off my observation but take this piece of advice my dad gave me, 'it's better to be pissed off than it is to be pissed on.' Let it go. However, I hope whatever's ailing you doesn't screw up our date. I've been working like a slave and I need to let my hair down to just be Zy tonight." I have learned to appreciate her eloquence. Yeah, I know I'm a thug, but when you fuck with women like the one in my passenger seat, you gotta step ya game up in the vocabulary department. (wink).

It just so happened that Maxwell crooned in the background and I liked the song, so I turned the radio up.

Your face will be the reason I smile,

But I will not see what I cannot have forever,

I'll always love ya, I hope you feel the same.

We both looked at each other and bobbed our heads to the same beat. What I heard next blew me away, my dick immediately rocked up.

"Oh you played me dirty, your game was so bad

You toyed with my affliction

Had to fill out my prescription

Found the remedy, I had to set you free,"

Zyyah belted out, signing the next verse, and I swear, she could've won any and all singing competitions. I stared at her, and she apologized. "Sorry about that, I just love Maxwell. I wanted to marry him when I was younger, then I grew up," she laughed.

"Don't apologize, you have the voice of the Herald Angels on high, girl. What are you ashamed of?"

"Well, now that you know one of my many secrets, tell me something about you," she smiled. I was breathless and still in awe of her melody.

"Hmmm, I hate to text people who don't reply but have their read receipt on. That really drives me crazy. Please don't ever do that. Have the common courtesy to either not check it if you can't respond or to turn that feature off, ya heard me?" I asked. She laughed causing me to laugh. "What's funny? That shit aggavatin'."

Buzz, buzz, buzz. My celly alerted me of a call. I looked at the screen to realize the fuckin nutcase apparently took me for a joke. Hitting the red ignore button, I placed my phone in the cupholder, facing the dash so neither of us could see the screen and drove off into the direction of out destination.

"I laughed because when I first moved here, when people would say 'Ya heard me' I would say 'Yes, I heard you' and they would explain that it was just a way of expressing passion about what was being said," we both laughed again. "Also, I know that you are a single man and you have your business to take care of, so please don't ignore calls on my account," she said with a genuine smile.

"Nah, I'm not answering the phone tonight. It's all about us getting to know each other a little better. My employees know how to handle business and everything else can wait, ya heard me," as the phrase left my lips, I chuckled. I guess since she pinpointed the statement, I became more aware of how often I used it. Eventually, I would get away from it altogether, it was not really an alluring phrase to constantly repeat.

"What is this place?" Zyyah asked as we pulled into the parking lot of a well-established Creole restaurant. I knew she would like this place, plus it belonged to an old friend of mine.

"It's called Commander's Palace, a fancy Creole restaurant, ya heard me. Sit tight, I will get your door," I told her.

Hopping out of the driver's side, I strutted over to her side and opened her door allowing her to step out of the truck. She looked like new money and she smelled even better. We walked in and were greeted immediately. I asked to be seated at a back corner table. Typically, they wouldn't seat you anywhere you asked due to it being by reservation only. Needless to say, I got rank up in ya, ya heard me.

It was crazy how much alike we were. Two peas from a totally different pod be we were on one accord. From the salad to the dessert we ordered the exact same shit. To give you a visual of what we ordered, just in case you were to visit one day, we had Ponchatoula Strawberry Salad, Boudin stuffed Quail, and for dessert we had Creole Bread Pudding Soufflé.

My phone wouldn't stop ringing in my pocket. Thinking it was one of the fellas, I decided to take it out and peek at it. "I know I said I wasn't gonna answer my phone, but I'mma look to see who keeps blowing me up. Ok?" I informed Zyyah. Just as my date was going good, the sight of this crazy hoe's number tried to creep in and ruin it.

Shaking it off, I decided to power my phone off. I stretched my long legs under the table and accidentally rubbed up against her leg. "My bad boo, I ain't tryna play footsies, we too old for that type of shit," I apologized.

I quit drinking a minute ago, but I told her that if she wanted a drink, it wouldn't bother me. I appreciated that she respected the fact, and agreed not to drink tonight. Because of that reason, when she stepped away to go to the bat'rum, I ordered her a bottle of *Au Bon Climat*, to go. It was the best tasting wine they had on the menu and it came in a nice looking ass bag. I was a Jameson man but, being close friends with the nigga who owned this place, I had my fair share of wine tasting.

"This place is amazing. Thank you for a great date, Jacques," Zyyah said after returning from the bat'rum. I stared at her, taking in all of her beauty. Sure, I had seen her before tonight, but it at was this very moment that I had truly taken in her absoluteness.

"Tonight is just getting started, boo. We are only a quarter of the way there. I'mma head to the bat'rum so we can go to the next destination," I informed her and her eyes lit up. I cruised my way to the watering hole. Just as I started to relieve myself, I heard the door open and close and thought nothing of it. Shortly after that, a set of skinny tattooed arms were wrapping around my waist from behind. I pissed all over the floor, while grabbing my forever bitch from the holster.

"Whoa, Kezzy Pooh. Why are you so on edge? It's just little ole me," Faye cooed. She reminded me of the bitch from the movie *Fatal Attraction*. "You should let me give you some head while I got you alone."

"Bitch, what the fuck are you doing here? How did you know that I was here and how did you get in? This place is by reservation only," I stated the obvious out of sheer contempt of her presence.

Her eyes were glossed over like a powder-head (cocaine addict) and her makeup was caked on like she was trying to hide something, maybe a black-eye. Whatever it was, I didn't give a fuck. Not my bitch, not my problem. As I attempted to walk around her to return to my date, the bitch latched on to me like her life depended on it. I had to pry her off of me, literally.

"Jacques, we are not done. I don't know what the fuck you thought but uh, you fuck with me, you stuck with me."

With those words the door opened, and she disappeared into the stall that she stood near. It was my cue to escape. I shot table.

"Are you ready to go?" I queried Zyyah, pressed for time.

"Are you ok? Oh my God, did something happen? Is Chyna ok?" Zyyah fired one question after another. Grabbing her coat, purse, and wine bag with swiftness, we speed walked up outta there so fast, I didn't remember if I had signed the receipt or left a tip.

$$$$

"So, what you're saying is, you eat peanuts but not peanut butter and oatmeal cookies but not oatmeal?" Zyyah giggled at my revelation. She laid on the blanket atop the grass and I had my head resting on her thick thigh. We were doing the twenty-one questions thing whilst staring at the dark skies that accompanied the calm waters on the Lakefront.

"C'mon now, you can't laugh remember, we promised not to make mockeries of each other's dark secrets," I scolded with a slight chuckle.

126

"Really, Jacques? You barely stopped laughing at the fact that my favorite singer is Kelly Clarkson and my favorite band is Journey," she reproached.

"I'm in a smoky room,
With the smell of wine
And cheap perfuuuume"

A nigga sang the line as best as I could. Unbeknownst to her, that song got me through plenty of nights being home alone.

"What do you know about that song? OMG, that's my favorite song of all time. I was teased as a teenager and it healed my heart many of nights. I had goals and aspirations of becoming a singer/songwriter. I gave up on it because of all of the negative comments I got about how I looked. I wasn't always this toned." There was a gravid pause, which caused me to look up at her. I noticed a tear rolling down her left cheek.

"Don't cry, bae. You gone make me wanna go fuck every muthafucka up that tried you, ya heard me," I wiped her cheek.

"I've always believed I was beautiful because of who I was on the inside. Yeah, I carried around more weight than most girls, but that didn't bother me until my sophomore year in college," she shook her head. "I had written a beautiful piece and sang with a melody that matched my soul. When the song was over there was only two people in the room with dry eyes. The professor and the girl he was having sex with. Needless to say, she won the competition for the scholarship to Berkley College of

Music." That revelation hurt my soul. It was fucked up man, this girl can blow.

We laid there staring into the sky for about fifteen minutes and I felt the chemistry burning between us.

"Can I kiss you?" I asked.

"I don't know, can you?" she responded with her smot-ass-mouf. I pinched her stomach causing her to giggle, that started a war because I tickled her, and she laughed until she was breathless.

I laid down beside her and stared at her face. She had dimples that were so deep I could bathe in them. She covered her face, and I didn't like the insecurity, so I pulled her hand away.

"Don't do that shit, bae. You can bare all with me. I know I'm a thug-ass nigga, and I'm prolly far from your type. But if you stick around long enough, you will find that I have a heart, yeah. "She released her breath and it smelled like a leaf of fresh mint. "Now, may I kiss your sexy ass or not?" I inquired again and bit my bottom lip.

"Yes," she said and nodded her head. I leaned in and put that tongue work on her ass. She wasn't a bad kisser.

Chapter 16 – Zyyah

"I could lay here forever. You make me feel so free," I said as I looked Jacques in his eyes. That kiss was breath-taking and his lips, Lord, his lips were so soft. I don't know if I expected them to be rough because of his demeanor, but the passion behind that kiss took me by surprise. Following that unforgettable kiss, he laid his head in my chest and it felt perfect.

"I need to let you know something," he stammered. I admit he had me nervous of what he'd reveal because he was so boisterous that I didn't take him for the coy, modest type.

"Should I be afraid of what you have to tell me?" I asked him.

Jacques looked away and blew out a long, hard breath. That triggered me to want to get up. I didn't know what he was about to tell me, but I had a gut-wrenching feeling, it wouldn't be good. I could feel my mood changing, I needed to get home and fast. I tried to roll him off of my chest so I could get up and head towards the truck, but he wouldn't allow me to move.

"Jacques, can you take me home, please?"

"I don't know, can I?" he countered back. I wasn't in a mood to play at that point. Therefore, I didn't laugh, giggle, chuckle, any of that. "Don't be like that bae, I need to tell you this, but I don't want you to run off on me like I'm the devil or some shit."

"Just say whatever it is, Jesus Christ! You are really messing with my nerves right now." I was on edge and he was trying my patience.

"Ok, I have never dated a woman in my entire adult life," he blurted out.

"Oh my God, are you gay? Did I just kiss a confused homosexual? So you wanna test the waters with me? What kind of crap is this? Ashton Kutcher, come out. I must be being punked!" Yelling the latter of my rant, I looked down at Jacques and he was laughing so hard his body shook. "I don't think any of this is funny, take me home! NOW!"

"Calm down, yeah. A nigga ain't gay, bruh. You trippin' for real, for real. I can't deal with the dramatics, ya heard me," he was still laughing at what I thought was testing my life.

"You just said that you haven't dated a woman in your adult life, so please explain. Unless you have been practicing celibacy, please do tell how you aren't gay. How Sway?"

"Ok, ok, I'mma tell you this once, so listen and stop jumping to conclusions man," he stared at me for confirmation to move forward with his revelation.

I motioned my hand in a roundabout way, "Ok, I'm listening."

"I haven't dated a female on a monogamous level since I got my heart broken by my first love, Tameka, in eighth grade. I haven't had the urge to be happy with another person because my only love is what I chase daily… money," he stared at me, I guess to feel me out before he continued. "It is very selfish and hellish of me, but I have only dated women who has something to lose, so that neither of us would become attached." He looked away from me, I guess he feared judgment or disappointment.

"I appreciate your honesty. There is nothing I can say about you being one-hundred percent with me so early in the game of friendship and trust-building. I don't have anything as drastic as that, but I can offer one more of my darkest secrets. Do you mind if we headed home, it's getting chilly out here on the water?" I asked.

"Sure, I'll take you home, Zyyah." Defeated was the vibe I got from him. He'd been referring to me as *bae* for some hours, now he's calling me by the name that my parents gave me. I truthfully didn't know how I felt about that. Standing to my feet and folding the blanket we laid on, I looked at him and for the first time since he revealed one of his truths. I noticed a profound sadness. We headed to the car, he opened the door, allowing me to get in first. After he got in, he started his truck, we buckled up, and he headed toward my apartment.

It was a very solemn ride. I wanted to hold him and let him know that I had not judged him by his disclosure, I just didn't know how to respond. I didn't care about his past, as long as he didn't care about mine.

Pulling into the same spot that he parked in to pick me up, he put his car in park without cutting the engine. He got out, walked around, opened my door and held his hand out to help me down. Once I gathered my things from the floorboard and shut the door, he gave me a hug.

"Thank you for one of the best nights this year, Zyyah."

"Where ya going?

Why you leaving so soon?

Is there somewhere else that is better for you?

What is love, if you're not here with me

What is love, if it's not guaranteed"

I belted out the lyrics from Veronika Bozeman's *What Is Love*. It wasn't that I loved him, because I barely knew him. I just wanted him to know that it was a lonely world and he didn't have to face it alone.

I looked into his eyes so that our souls could connect. I needed him to feel my presence.

"Don't think I am holding against you what you let me in on. We are at a dating stage, and because you have trusted me with a few of your secrets, I'd like to invite you up to my apartment. Would you like to come up for something to drink or to watch a movie?"

He looked at me side-eyed.

"I don't do pity parties, bruh. Don't invite me up because you feel sorry for me," he told me with every ounce of seriousness ever-present on his handsome face. His lips were moving, and I was staring as he licked them and talked. The slight gap between his two front teeth was sexy to me. I hadn't heard a word after 'feel sorry for me.' *Bad kitty, down girl, not tonight. We will not give him a whorish impression,* I thought.

He waved his hand before my face, "Earth to Zyyah, hello!" he yelled.

"I apologize, I zoned out for a second. Why do you think I have pity for you? I simply wanted to know if you wanted to come up because I still haven't told you what I wanted to say at the Lake. I mean, if you don't want to know, or are afraid to come up, it's totally fine," I responded, finally coming out of the transfixion that his lips had me in.

"Shiii, you got the game fucked up, yeah. I ain't never been scared of nothing in my life, ya heard me. Let me lock my truck up. I hope you got good stuff because you not finna use my body up with the *Netflix and Chill* shit. My sex ain't easy to get. Ha, ha, ha," he laughed.

"You are so freaking silly. I don't want your sex. I'm only interested in your mental right now. And even if I did, you couldn't deny all of this woman," I flirted back and immediately regretted my word choice. We walked through the pathway into my building which was located opposite the office, on the other side of the pool. I placed my key in the door and welcomed him in.

"Smack in the middle of the complex, huh?" Jacques asked.

"Yeah, but I told you that already," I recalled.

"This is nice, Z. I see you into jungle themes, huh? You got a lil' wild animal tamed in here somewhere?" he asked as he looked around.

He searched as if he was looking to see if a little tiger would be running wild. Who did he think I was, Antoine Yates' sister?

"Thank you. Have a seat, silly. Make yourself at home while I gather our snacks," I responded and giggled at his wild animal comment. I went into the kitchen, "What do you want to drink? I have tea, lemonade, ginger ale, Kool-Aid, wa—"

"What kind of Kool-Aid?" he cut me off.

"It's grape mixed with lemonade, don't judge me!" I laughed.

"That's my shit, let me get a tall glass on the rocks, ya heard me!" he responded. We were literally more alike than anyone I'd ever met.

I poured each of us a glass. I grabbed the tortilla chips and the spinach and artichoke dip, placed it all on a serving tray and headed out. Deciding to grab the jalapeño cheese dip, I turned around and grabbed that, placed it on the tray and headed to the living room. I sat opposite of him and placed my left leg under my body. Grabbing the remote, I powered on the entertainment center, and intuitively scrolled through my recordings to see what I had to catch up on.

"Oooh, I'm three episodes behind, I really need to catch up," I mumbled to myself as I stopped scrolling once I reached *Grey's Anatomy*.

"We can watch Grey's if you want. But first, you got something to tell me, right?" he questioned. I was avoiding this like the plague. I had never told anyone this secret, not even Deja, and she knew almost everything about me.

I took a deep breath, trying to put all of my fears in a box.

"Well, when I was a junior in college, I had fallen in love with a guy who was several years older than I was. I had been doubling as a Music major with a Psychology minor, so I was busting my behind, mindlessly running around campus. One day I was running behind, and like a scene from a movie, I had run smack into *him* and my things fell everywhere," I paused to gather myself.

"Overwhelmed by mid-terms, I kneeled to gather my crap and the tears rolled freely, it was like I needed to cleanse my soul. *He* was helping me pick up my things, *he* realized I was crying so *he* pulled his handkerchief from his pocket and wiped my tears." Reliving that moment had almost brought me to a weak moment. I fought it and kept going with my truth. "I thanked him for the helping hand and made my way to class. It was my last class of the day." Finally gazing at Jacques, I noticed his demeanor had softened as he listened attentively. This guy had to be the most unpredictable person I'd met in my life.

"After blustering through my exam, I scurried back through Arizona State University's campus trying to get to my car. I just wanted to sleep the rest of the day away. Low and behold, the same guy stopped me in the courtyard. We exchanged numbers and from there we dated until mid-way through my first year of grad school," I half-smiled.

"I don't see what's so dark and secretive about that, it sounds like a great love story," Jacques cut in.

"Well, *he* took my virginity after seven months of dating. Of course, *he* had me under the assumption that he was an engineering student. We worked out together, did study hall, and ate lunch in the courtyard. The latest *he* would stay out with me was ten-thirty. Me, not thinking beyond early classes, I had no objections because my first class was at seven-thirty a.m.," pausing again, I thought of how gullible I was. Yet again, I shook back my tears.

"Are you ok, bae?" There was the pet name again. Hearing that warmed my heart and gave me will to continue.

"I'm great. Let me finish, ok. This is something that I have been harboring for a long time." Asking him to stop interrupting in the most relaxed way I knew how, he looked at me intently.

"The floor is yours," he replied.

"Thank you, Hun. So, we went through my junior and senior year as the power couple, I thought. It was graduation and I showed up to be fitted for my cap and gown. My English One professor from my freshman and sophomore years was in charge of capping. I walked up to her and she stared at me. I was like Mrs. Jones, don't you remember me? It's me Zyyah, Zyyah Hollins. The student that sat at the front of class and admired your wedding ring for two semesters. She was like, 'Oooh child, I knew your face looked familiar, did you change your hair?' I said yes, that and, I lost seventy pounds." No longer able to hold back my tears, Jacques grabbed my hand and squeezed, but he didn't utter a word.

"She said 'well, only love can do that to you, and for you baby girl, give me a hug'. And I did. As we broke our hug a familiar voice came up behind me, 'Baby, you know everybody on campus, don't you?' Cutting between us, they embraced in a very passionate kiss. Pushing him back, she said, 'Erich, I want you to meet one of my favorite students, the one I bragged about two years ago.' When *he* turned around my mouth dropped, and his eyes pleaded with me to keep my mouth shut." The dam had broken. Jacques grabbed tissues from the box on the coffee table, still not saying a word.

I gathered myself and continued. "Needless to say, I kept my mouth shut and went with the formalities as *he* introduced himself as Professor Jones, the Dean of the Engineering Department. We finished up the fitting and I went on my way. I couldn't compose myself once I exited the conference room where the fitting was held." Looking at Jacques, I knew he was pissed. The look in his eyes were that of the inferno of Hell.

"After two weeks of calls, text messages, and leaving messages with my roommate, I finally returned Erich's call. I fell for all the bull-crap *he* sent my way, for all of the empty promises. I had become one of his best-kept secrets and I was ok with it until I found out I wasn't his only mistress and threatened to leave," I shook away my tears as I thought of how low of a woman I had become for this man.

Jacques wiped my tears for support. "We sat in his car outside of campus housing and I told him that I could no longer be a part of his coterie of mistresses. When I told him that, *he* grabbed me by my hair and mushed my head against the passenger side window, causing my forehead to split. With blood leaking down the side of my face, *he* forced me to perform oral sex on him." With that Jacques squeezed my hand a bit harder.

"Ow, ow, ouch, Jacques! Let me go!" I cried and snatched my hand from the death-grip.

"Oh, Bae, I didn't realize I was squeezing you that hard. I envisioned my hands wrapped around Erich bitch ass neck. I'm so sorry, I would never intentionally harm you. You gotta believe me, ya heard me," Jacques kissed my hand multiple times, causing me to laugh. "What's so funny?" he asked.

"You're kissing my hand like Pepe Le Pew." We both laughed.

"Shut that ass up, I just wanted to make it better. Continue," he suggested.

Feeling like I had to play it safe, I kindly took my hand away. "After that *he* threatened to send nude pictures that *he* had taken of me, to the athletic department, anonymously. Both fortunately and unfortunately, *he* had done the same thing to a few other students and they reported him. I can't believe that you're the first and only person I have ever shared this with." I looked at Jacques to try and gauge his emotion, but failed.

"That's it? What happened to that bitch ass nigga, bae? What the fuck, man. Ok they reported him, what else, that can't be the end. I'm gonna kill that muthafucka," Jacques seethed with anger.

"*He* ended up in prison with ninety-nine years. *He* was a part of a sex trafficking operation. The girls ranged from ages thirteen to twenty-one. Also, a few of my alumni came forward with rape allegations that *he* was found guilty of. Not long after *he* was locked up in Florence, AZ prison, *he* was found dead with a broomstick up his anus," I cringed.

"I'm glad you survived and finally released this burden. Otherwise, I woulda neva been sitting here witcha," Jacques admitted. "Let's watch Grey's. I'm only one episode behind, but I'll watch the other two again. I love me some Miranda Bailey, with her cute, bossy, thick ass," I hit him on the arm and he kissed the side of my face. "I'mma put a throw pillow on your lap and lay down. Is that cool, Bae?" he queried.

"Yep, let's go, Grey's fan…," he laid on his back, with his head in my lap. It was the first time I realized he had taken his shoes off. Who knew that a hardened thug had a heart, and a love for nighttime soap operas.

Chapter 17 - Chyna

I was so tired, I'd been planning for my first annual Christmas party from home. Although I knew Casey had everything under control, I wanted to be hands on. The party was for family and close friends and by invitation only. I hadn't been to the office since the shooting and had not planned on going back there. However, Ju'an had other plans for me. He told me that we were going to face whatever obstacles we had, together. Nothing and no one would keep us from our livelihoods. I had been onboard until the time presented its self.

He mentioned that he'd met Faith. Come to find out he was the guy with the unique name that showed up as a patient, at his office not too long ago. He would be returning for an appointment next month. I had spoken with Hope once since the hospital. However, we had been texting. I don't think Ju'an liked it, but I wanted to get to know my little brothers. Hope had texted me a pic of himself and his twin, the resemblance between us was beyond freaky. We were the olive versions of Pappi.

"Hey baby, how are you today?" Ju'an walked in and interrupted my thoughts.

"I'm good, bae. What's up with you? You're here early," I mentioned, looking at the time.

"Yeah, I had no more patients after ten, so I packed up and came home, hoping to get some mid-day sex. I miss that good-stuff," the mention of that three-letter word caused a flood in the valley. We hadn't made love since I was released from the hospital. That was almost two weeks ago.

"I would love to oblige, however, I am meeting Hope for lunch today. Would you like to join?" letting him down as easy as I could, he looked confused.

"What do you mean you are meeting Hope for lunch? I don't trust that nigga. I told you that I have a feeling that your dad and them boys are behind the drive-by," he yelled. "Chy, all this sneaky shit ain't gone work. What if that nigga out to harm you?"

"Sha, I'mma need you to lower your tone when you're talking to me. Don't get the game misconstrued. I'm pregnant, not stupid. We're not gonna start this type of shit. We haven't been disrespectful to each other and we not gonna do this," I countered back, giving him as much shit as he gave me.

Grabbing my purse and keys, I headed toward the door. I didn't know if I was more hurt that he talked to me like a two-bit whore or upset that he spoke to me like he didn't know who the hell I was.

"Chyna, don't leave mad, Bae," he came up behind me closing the door. "I apologize for speaking to you that way. I just have a bad feeling about this. I'm not going to intrude, just be careful and please take your pistol," he kissed my forehead and hugged me around my waist.

"I love you, baby, and you know that I love me too. You don't have to worry. We are gonna play it safe, we gotta protect our legacy, our unborn," I returned his gesture and kissed his lips.

"Who is we, why do you keep saying we?" he asked confused.

"Me and Ghi," I responded causing him to look at me like I had lost my damn mind.

I pulled my new Glock 9mm with Ghi's picture airbrushed on the grip. He smiled and smacked my ass. Walking me to the car, he opened and closed my door. I rolled my window down and gave him another kiss before getting buckled in and driving off.

I arrived at my destination in less than thirty minutes. I finally found parking a half a block away from Pascal's Manale, known to the native's as Pascal's. The unborn couldn't wait to get inside, we had been craving the shrimp and grits since Hope mentioned that he wanted to meet there. The aroma made me so hungry, I couldn't get there fast enough. I stalked into the direction of the restaurant.

"Sis," I heard a voice call out. I looked over my shoulder and recognized my brother standing near a Buick. His smile was so big that I could feel his heart exuding through it genuinely. "Is it ok if I give you a hug?" he questioned.

I was leery, but I obliged. "Of course, baby bro. Bring it in," I laughed. After releasing our embrace, he stared at me, making me feel indifferent about him being genuine. "Why are you looking at me crazy?" I queried.

"I'm taking in the beauty of my big sis and you all smelling like new money and shit. I can't believe how much twin looks like you," he replied, which caused me to laugh.

"If you guys are twins, shouldn't we all look alike," I responded still laughing. "Let's go inside, silly, I'm starving. I'm eating for two now, but of course you know that already."

"Congrats on your new bundle. I don't remember you saying you was pregnant though, sis," Hope said. That caused me to second-guess my mental state. I would bet my last dollar that I had told him.

Blowing off the miscommunication, I linked my arm inside of his, and we continued our short walk to the restaurant. Once we got inside and were seated we ordered sweet tea to drink, calamari for the appetizer and we both had the barbecue shrimp. I had mine with grits and Hope had his as a sandwich.

"So why didn't Faith come? I thought you was gonna bring him, so we can all sit down and get to know each other," I questioned between bites of calamari.

"Damn sis, I didn't take you for the kind to talk with food in your mouth. That's pretty rude, don't you think?" he countered.

"Typically, I wouldn't but like I said outside, I'm starving and I don't really have time to sit here. I'm having my Christmas party tonight, so I have appointments to get to. I need my nails, make-up, and hair done and I gotta pick my dress up by six," I informed him, never apologizing for my rudeness.

"If you got all that shit to do, why did you agree to meet me today? I could've been up in some pussy right now, ya heard me sis?" He responded with a mouthful of food. It was gross the way his food fell from his mouth back onto his plate.

"You know, little bro, you're right. I agreed to meet you, but I had no idea the meeting would go this way. You are totally different in person than you are over the phone," Grabbing the waitress's attention as she passed by, I asked for the bill and a to go plate for my food.

"I don't need you to pay for my shit, I can hold my own. Actually, I can hold it down for you too. You can bounce, I will handle the ticket," he blew me off.

"You are truly your father's son, you are one rude motherfucker. I really wanted you guys to come to my party tonight. If you think you can check your attitude at the door, here is the invitation for you and Faith." Slamming the invitation on the table along with thirty dollars. Leaving before the waitress came back with a to-go plate, I made my exit.

Unable to hold my emotions, I sat in my car and cried like I had lost my best friend, all over again. Deciding against calling Ju'an, I called Kez instead.

"So, I found out that I have nineteen-year-old twin brothers while I was in the hospital," I informed Kez as I calmed down enough to talk and drive into the direction of the nail shop.

"Oh, word? That's what's up. How do you feel about it?" he replied.

"I'm not sure how I feel. At first, I was excited but after meeting with one of them today, I don't think I wanna be a part of their lives," I said.

"Damn sis, it was that bad huh?"

"Indeed, I can't believe he was so rude. He wasn't like that on the phone and his text were so sweet," I said into the Bluetooth as I sat getting my nails done.

"C'mon Chy, you know text don't have a tone, so you can't really judge by that," Kez responded, trying to reason with me. "I mean, you know I'm bout that life, I will fuck his lil' ass up if that's what you want," he continued.

"I know you would but calm down, there was just something different about him. All around. I don't wanna tell Ju'an because he tried to keep me from meeting with him earlier. He said he didn't trust them and that he felt they, along with Pappi, had something to do with the situation at my building when I got shot," I felt the need to let him know so he wouldn't go flapping his lips to Ju'an. "I gave him an invite to come to the party tonight."

"What's their names sis? In case I gotta fuck they lil' asses up I wanna know, ya heard me," we laughed. Needless to say, Kez was serious.

146

"The one I met up with today, his name is Hope and the oth— Let me hit you back that's Ju'an calling in," I was cut off by my other line beeping in my ear.

$$$$

Pulling up to my building, I felt panic take over. I was hyperventilating, I needed a bag to breathe into. Where was a damn inhaler when I needed one? I couldn't think, breathe, or move as I stared at the front of the newly bricked building. The very spot that I had been shot two weeks ago to date. Yeah, Ju'an had the contractors come through to change the exterior of the building, but it didn't change what I felt inside. I was afraid, an emotion that rarely presented itself inside of me. My palms were sweaty and when I looked in the mirror, so was my forehead.

Tap. Tap. Tap. I flinched, then looked out of the driver side window and acknowledged a smiling Casey. I rolled my window down. "Hey Sha, I'm just touching up my lip gloss," I lied. I didn't know how long she had been standing there.

"Boss lady, are you gonna get out or are you gonna host the party from the driver seat of your car?" She asked genuinely. "It's going to be fine, let's go inside."

"Easy for you to say, you didn't get shot," I snapped.

"That's fair, you're right. Maybe it was an insensitive suggestion, however you didn't have to be so rude. You showed up today. I assumed you had placed your fears and doubts of returning on the back burner," Casey snapped back. "I've never viewed you as weak or a prisoner of your own fear. Get your ass out of the car and come into the building so we can get this party started!" she demanded.

One thing about Casey that I loved and hated, was her ability to put someone in their place and never miss a beat. Even though she worked for me, she was no holds barred, I could get it too.

Realizing she was right, I decided to get out of the safety of my car to enter my building. *I'm Chyna-Sinc Naeema Green, I run my life. I am woman, hear me roar,* I thought as I took a deep breath. "I apologize Casey, and bitch you're fired. Not any time soon, but you are." Hooking her arm inside of mine, we laughed and headed in, although I was still uncomfortable.

Chapter 18 – Naomi Green

"Oh, this bitch think she just get to cut me off after getting me adapted to a nice lifestyle. I don't know who the fuck she thought she was fucking with, but I'm gonna show up and show out at that fuckin party. I guess she so busy she didn't notice I was following all of her social media accounts, and since she brags to the world about everything, I know her every move," I said as I talked to my man.

"It's called social status not bragging. Nonetheless, I'm gone be right by your side just in case that soft, dentist hands, having nigga try to step to you like a damn fool. If they want peace, tell them you will leave for ten g's, no problems," he responded while popping the tourniquet from his arm.

"Nigga, that boy gone beat the shit outta your loaded ass. You getting too full, baby. We not gone be able to strong arm nobody with your head in the clouds," I said to him.

Whap! Whap! Whap!

James lit my ass up in a matter of seconds. He smacked me in my head, my face, and followed-up with a flurry of body blows. I didn't know why I continuously tested his patience when he was full of that shit. He thought he was immortal when we shot up our heroin and my emasculation of him due to his drug addiction, apparently pissed him off.

He had been beating my ass so much since Chyna-Sinc put me out, I had grown accustomed to it. I ignored my swelling eye and tied my arm up to finish off my peanut sack (small baggie of heroin).

I sat there in a doped-out daze for mere minutes before being hit with a bright idea. "Why don't we ask them motherfuckers for a hundred K? It ain't like they ain't got it." At the mention of a hundred thousand dollars, James' eyes grew larger as he sobered up.

"A hunnit K would set us up, baby. We can find us a lil' pad and stop squatting in these abandoned houses like the rest of these homeless muthafuckas. We are better than them," he stated cockily. "Every time you suck a nigga dick for our fix, it makes me feel like I'm less than a man."

When he said that, I looked at him and wanted to respond. I knew how to pick my battles, so I'll save that fight for another day.

I was glad that the house had working lights and running water. I was able to clean up and get ready for the Christmas party. After two hours had passed, we headed out towards Chyna's office. In route, I spaced out.

"Do you wanna fuck me or not?" I asked Renard.

"Man, hell naw! I don't want no parts of that," he said as he motioned his hand toward my body, in an up and down manner. "You're Sin's woman. Not only is he the craziest Cajun I ever met, he's my boss, and you're off limits. I wouldn't dare cross him by sleeping with you. He trusts me with his business affairs and apparently his wife and

child. He sent me to look after you and Chyna because he couldn't leave the cleaners."

"What the fuck you mean by look after us? I don't need nobody looking after me, I'm a grown ass woman," I said and grabbed his dick. "You gone fuck this pussy and break me off a few grams of that brown sugar?"
He smacked my hand away so hard I wanted to tell Sinclair he hit me. I knew Sin would've killed him so instead I offered him something I knew he wouldn't refuse. "Since you don't want my pussy thinking it's ran through, take Chyna. Her little three-year-old pussy is pure and untouched. You can have it, I need my fuckin fix, Ren."

"So you're willing to risk baby Chyna's innocence and purity for a hit of that smack?" he asked. He looked at me slyly, I knew I had piqued his interest. I figured he was either gay or into children since he didn't wanna fuck me. Everybody wanted to fuck me, "I'll take her," he said. I freely handed her over in exchange for ten packs.
After he pulled off with Chyna, I headed inside to get full. Nodding off after my fourth peanut sack, a wave of anxiety came over me, causing my heart to race. I threw up, then fell asleep. Within what felt like moments, I was awakened by a bucket of cold water being splashed in my face. Sinclair stood there red as a crawfish, yapping his

mouth. I couldn't understand shit he said because when
he was pissed every other word was broken French.
"I'm gon take you home nah, Sha. Tomorrow, you outta
our life for good, yeah. You have taken dis shit too far
tryna sell our daughter for dope, ya done coo-yon," he
said causing me to laugh. I was higher than heaven's
ceiling.

"Earth to Naomi. Bitch, you can be over there thinking about that big dick nigga you be fucking for our dope if you want. That nigga don't want ya dope fiend ass," James yelled, breaking me out of my trance. I had been thinking about the day I was ripped from Chyna quite often. I wasn't affected by it, at least I didn't think I was.

"Ain't nobody thinking bout that, I'm thinking bout a plan for when we get inside," I lied. I couldn't believe I had stooped low enough to let a nigga fuck my daughter. Now here I was about to double cross her for money when she had been nothing but kind and loving. *Who gives a fuck?* I laughed and shook away the thought. "Knowing little Miss Prissy, we might not be able to get in without an invitation or being on the guest-list."

"Fuck the doubt shit, we gone get in and get our money, or we gonna make a scene and ruin her fuck ass party," James responded. "Let's head in!" We headed toward the front entrance with the rest of the party goers.

As we made our way to the door, the guy stopped us from walking in. "Excuse me, do you have an invitation?" he asked.

"No, we already been here we just went out to smoke," I responded quickly.

"If that's the case ma'am, may I see your wristband for re-entry?" he acted like a well-trained puppy.

"Look lil' boy, I'm Naomi Green, Chyna-Sinc's mother, now let me in this muthafuckin place before I make her fire your fake ass," I said to the pissy-tail child that stood before me.

"Ma'am, I can't let you in. Chyna has strict rules. No one in without an invitation, and I need my job," he stood his ground.

"Chyna-Sinc, tell this lil' boy to let your mother in this fucking building!" I yelled. James tried to barge his way in, causing two buff dudes to come out of nowhere. They handled his ass like the dope fiend he was. It was amusing to see him being handled the way he did me in his dope fits. I wouldn't dare allow him to see a glimmer of excitement in my eyes though, I knew better than that shit.

"What's going on here?" I heard Chyna's voice cutting through all of the commotion.

"Chyna-Sinc, baby let us in. It's Christmas, have a heart… please!" I begged. I know I sounded desperate, but I didn't give a fuck. I needed to do what I had to do to get close enough to get what I needed to get, MONEY!

I should be trying to make amends for almost ruining her life when she was a baby, but I lost my life when I chose Sinclair and his baby over the love of my family. Somebody had to pay, who better than her. I knew better than to fuck with Sin. Moving to New Orleans was the worst thing I had ever done. Everything moved too fast for a country girl like myself. If anything, Sinclair is the reason I'm so fucked up.

"Naomi, I'mma let you and whatever his name is in on one condition," she stated with a frown. I can't stand her saditty ass. Her father got her fucked up in the head.

"Here you go with your rules, Miss Prissy," I responded. With that, she turned her nose up and walked off. "Chyna come back, you know I was just kidding."

Saying whatever I need to say to get inside, I held in my anger that raged within the pit of my gut.

"Look, I'mma let you and that thing you call a man in, as long as either of you don't come in here being extra," she commanded.

"C'mon James, she's letting us in," I told my guy friend who was still fighting a losing battle with security.

"Let me go, stupid ass bitches. Y'all lucky I didn't wanna embarrass y'all in front of your boss and coworkers. Get the fuck off me." James' dope head ass swear he could beat anybody. In all honesty, he could only beat me. I had witnessed him get whooped on several times in the three years we had been together.

After we got inside, James made me stuff my purse with food. Before we left the house we were staying in, he made sure I had plenty of doubled grocery bags because we didn't have Tupperware or Ziploc bags.

154

"Chyna, can I speak to you, please?" Suppressing my hatred for her, I plastered on a smile.

"What do we have to talk about, Naomi?" She sounded as vindictive and hatful as I felt.

"I need to speak with you in private. You can't even hear me with all this loud ass be-bop music playing." Not wanting Ju'an's punk ass to know what was going on until he needed to, I needed to get Chyna alone. She was so damn gullible, I knew I could convince her to cut me a check.

"Ok Naomi, let's go to my office." Looking around to see who was watching, she led the way. Once we made it to the confines of her beautifully decorated office, which I had never seen, I laid it on her thick.

"Chyna-Sinc, I know I left on a bad note, but I really need you to come through for me baby girl," I played nice, so I could get her stupid ass in my corner.

"Naomi, this is my Christmas party, can't this wait?" she responded.

"No Chyna, this can't wait. I'm homeless. When you put me out, I had no one and nowhere to go. James is broke, he doesn't have shit but the car he drives around." Lord please don't let him be outside the door listening. The thought of the ass whooping he would put on me for hearing me speak ill of him, willed tears to spring from my eyes. I needed those tears to smooth her over, win her heart, and get in her good graces.

"Oh, Naomi, why didn't you just say something? Have you been homeless since you left?" I was working her ass, I watched the transition of her face from hate to love before my eyes. *Duck ass hoe.*

"I found a place," I informed her through sniffles. "All I need is a hundred thousand dollars and it's all mine," I told her and immediately I knew that amount was far-fetched.

"A HUNDRED THOUSAND DOLLARS?" she yelled. "Who the hell do you think you are to storm in here after several weeks with such a demand. Oh, did you believe you were able to hide the beatings that that fucking crackhead out there has been handing you with make-up? Did he put you up to this? I was willing to give you five K, but now, you can't have five dollars. Are you on that shit, too?" Chyna saw right through the stupid act. I couldn't believe she caught on so fast.

"I need this muthafuckin money, or I'm a dead woman. I'll take fifty K and be out of your life forever," I rebutted.

"Ha, ha, ha, ha! You can't be serious, right?" she questioned. I was enraged. I started scratching my arm, which caused my sleeve to raise, exposing my tracks from the recent needle marks.

"Bitch, I will tear this pretty little office up if you don't cut that damn check right now. It ain't gonna hurt your deep ass pockets. We all weren't lucky enough to snag a dentist and have a drug-dealing daddy. So what, James is a dope fiend that beats

156

my ass? He loves me." Pissed off, I looked around to see where I would start my tantrum.

"Get the fuck out of my place Naomi, before I embarrass your ass," she responded, further pissing me off.

Crash! Crash!

I slapped the picture of her and her bitch ass boyfriend off of her desk. It was secured inside of a beautiful Tiffany frame. Immediately after that, I slapped the picture of that whore Marilyn Monroe off of the wall. As if it was on cue, in busted James followed by some big red-boned bitch.

"Casey, get Ju'an and Kez" Chyna yelled.

"We already here. What's good, sis? The fuck's going on in this bitch? What up James, it's been a lil' minute. You still sucking on that glass dick or you stepped it up when you started playing with the heroin addict?" Jacques said as he grabbed my arm, exposed my track marks, and shook his head.

Damn, I would suck and fuck the shit outta his young, mean, sexy ass, I thought.

Chapter 19 – Jap

After all the shit Naomi had put Chy through, she had the nerve to show up demanding money. Not a lil' bit of money either, fifty damn K which had been reduced from the initial hunnit. Who the hell did she think she was fucking with? Apparently, she hadn't done her research. James uglass knew me and Kez well. Obviously, he wasn't aware that I was Chyna's man.

"We right chere, sis. What's good James?" Kez questioned the crackhead turned heroin addict that we knew since we were knee-high to a duck's ass. Old head used to sing for a fix. Back in the day, we called his ass J-Blues.

"James, you just gonna stand there and let this pissy-dick nigga grab all on me like that? I told you her punk-ass, soft-hand, dentist ass boyfriend and his wannabe thug ass brother would barge in trying to put a stop to our business matters. She is too weak to handle her own," Naomi's dope-head ass stated. I tried to warn Chy about her, but I would never throw that in her face for the reason that I'm not only a man, but her man. Plus, I was never one to say, "I told you so."

"L-l-l-look at y'all boys. Y'all done growed up on Ol' J-Blues, huh?" he stuttered over his words. The expression on Naomi's face was as priceless as the one I had caused during our last encounter.

"Say bruh, I don't have time for the small talk. Riddle me this shit, though," Kez confronted James.

"W-w-what you say, young buck?" he responded. That nigga was sweating like a hooker in church.

"You coming in here to basically rob my sis-in-law with her fuck ass moms. So, with the money that you thought you would get, was you planning on paying me my issue for the shit you ran out with a minute ago?" Kez rubbed his chin. After thinking about the hit we took because of that front we trusted him with, I decided to step in.

"I-I-I didn't know this was you, young buck." Sweat beads formed on his forehead as he pointed to Chy. "I clare to God, I woulda neva been in ya with this money-hungry bitch, and that's on the fa sho. It was all her idea to try and fuck her daughter outta a hunnit K."

Whap, pop, pop, whap!

After I smacked James in the head, I hit him with a right and left hook, then slapped him across the face with a hard left. With the commotion going on, I hadn't noticed Casey working Naomi's ass in the corner.

"Bitch, don't you ever come at my boss while she's carrying a child. You got life and bullshit all the way fucked up. Fuck you thought, hoe!" Casey was pissed. She had stomped a mudhole in Naomi's ass.

Attempting to pull Casey off of Naomi's ass, Chyna warned me against it. I guess that ass whipping was warranted and deemed overdue. Kez had had enough after about two more minutes. He finally stopped Casey by pulling her up and out of the corner. He placed her next to Chy as she regained control of her breathing.

"I'm sorry, boss lady." Casey's eyes pleaded for forgiveness. "I know she's your mom, but no one will disrespect or attack you in my presence. Not now, not ever!" She was furious.

When I saw Chy's reaction, I was saddened. Chyna stared at Naomi with hatred in her eyes as she hugged her colleague and friend and let the river overflow.

"Never in life do I want to see you again, Naomi. To think, I was ecstatic when you returned. I feel like such a damn fool to assume your return was genuine." Chy shook her head and the tears continued to fall. "Get them out of here. NOW!"

"Bitch, you ain't Sinclair. You ain't made of the same composition of neither of us, with your weak ass. You think you can just kick me out of your life, I'll be back," Naomi addressed Chyna. "And you, you big red bitch, I will see you again one day, and you best be ready," she talked shit, but never made eye contact with Casey.

"You know what they say, old school, two mountains will never meet but two people damn sure will. I'll be looking forward to tagging that ass again. Anyone wanting to attend that MAJOR event, will need to sign an N.D.A., bitch." Casey was ready to unleash again but Kez held her back.

160

"Looking at chu in comparison to Casey, you might wanna walk your eighty-five-pound ass outta ya," Kez suggested.

"What the fuck you mean by that, lil' boy?" Naomi quizzed with a lustful look in her eyes.

"You look like you pretty fucked up and Casey ready to go back downstairs to party. Call me a lil' boy again and I'mma cut her loose to finish dog-walking yo' ass," Kez laughed at Naomi's expense.

Gladly everything popped off inside of Chyna's office, therefore the partygoers were unaware of the events that had just transpired. I hate dealing with ignorance, it turns me into a back peddler. I don't like the thug that resides inside of me; when ignorance is bliss, Jap the Trapper rears his ugly head.

After gathering ourselves, Kez headed back to his date, who he had left with Toy. It was crazy to see how he was changing right before us. Happiness really did look good on my brother.

"I knew something was up when I saw J-Blues standing outside ya door so I signaled for Jap and Kez." Casey said as she hugged Chy. "You gone be alright, Chyna?" Casey asked as she broke their embrace.

"Yeah Sha, I'mma be ok. Thank you for having my back, friend."

"Always chick, you know I love to throw these hands. Bitches be having me fucked up thinking because I'm a pretty chick, I can't fight. Try again, bih!" They laughed. "I'mma head back downstairs, love." Casey left, closing the door behind her. She literally left looking the same way she came.

My baby looked so distraught, all I wanted to do was console her. I wanted to take her home and dick her down to make all of this shit go away.

"Thank God, you guys were here. Who knows what those dope fiends would've done to me," Chy sniffled.

I walked over to the door and locked it. She looked at me through tears with lust-filled eyes. I bit my bottom lip as I stared at the beauty that was growing my seed. *I'm about to do some damage to that pussy,* I thought as I walked over to her. As I stood chest to breast with her, I grabbed a handful of her thick mane and pulled her head back slightly. I devoured her neck, knowing it was her weak spot. I grabbed her breast with my free hand and squeezed it in a milking motion.

"Ju'an" was all she could get out.

"Shhhh! Let me take your mind off the shit that just popped off. You know the baby is hungry for growth, let me feed 'em," I whispered against the side of her face.

"Who said it's a him?" she questioned between breaths. Her breathing became rugged, that's when I went in for the kill.

The dress she was wearing gave me full access to all of her. I pulled the titty out that I was fondling with and popped it in my mouth like a newborn. Picking her up, I carried her over to the sofa that was conveniently inside of her office and exposed her beautiful apple bottom. Her juices visibly soaked her panties, the sight immediately rocked me up. I rubbed her kitten, causing a constant flow. I stuck my finger inside and pulled it out. Sticking it in my mouth, the taste of her essence was sweet as a peach. I could no longer hold back.

Ripping her panties from her body, I took my time with my woman. Given the environment we were in, I still made her feel like she was my queen and I, her king. I took my time finessing the pussy. After some time had passed and we had both been relieved of our sexual tension, we went into the adjoining bathroom and washed up.

As if it was on cue, as soon as we walked out of the bathroom, there was a knock at the door. Chyna looked at me with a satisfied but embarrassed look, as if whoever was on the other side of the door knew what we had just done.

Opening the door and stepping to the side, in walked Casey. "Why y'all look like... You know what, never mind." She looked at us sideways with a smirk on her face. "There's a guy named Hope looking for you. He says he's your brother?" she said it more as a question than a statement. She looked utterly confused. "He does kind of look like you, but I never heard anything about a brother," she finished, smiled at the both of us, and headed out.

"She knows," Chyna smiled and popped my arm.

"Of course she knows, babe. How else did you get pregnant?" I asked and embraced her in a passionate kiss. "Let's go see what this fool wants," I said with every bit of distrust as possible. I refused to hide my true feelings because I wasn't that dude. I didn't like any of her family, but I loved her.

"Play nice baby, please," Chyna begged.

"Um-hmh!" I half-agreed.

We walked down the steps, and as soon as we rounded the corner, I looked toward the entrance and noticed a dude that was the exact replica of Chyna. As I looked near the bar, I saw Kez looking in the same direction. What hadn't went unnoticed was the look of death in his eyes. I knew shit was about to pop off, but I prayed that it didn't. Chyna didn't need any more stress tonight.

Chapter 20 – Kez

Man, ain't this some fuck shit. Last weekend, I had the best night of my life only to come out to my truck keyed and sitting on three flats. This week, I see the nigga that I believe robbed me and gave me a concussion. I know sis 'bout to be mad as fuck at me for ruining her party, but this nigga ain't gone walk up outta ya.

I didn't tell my lil' rounds what I was headed to do because I knew they would flash out, talm bout I needed to chill and all that other pussy shit. I had just witnessed a smack fest and a good old-fashioned catfight. Well, technically it was an ass whipping. The heroin addict didn't hold a match to Casey. Looking at her, I wouldn't have guessed she threw them dogs like that, but that bitch was bad as Laila Ali. I would bet money on her any day of the week.

Heading over to meet up with my assumed adversary, I noticed Jap and Chy walking in his direction. Seeing Chy and this nigga in the same room, I noticed the resemblance. That nigga must be one of the twin brothers she told me about. Apparently, he was the one she met up with earlier today. *Am I really that fucked up in the head about revenge?*

In route, I realized it was too late to change directions, so I continued to walk past them pretending to go outside to smoke. The closer I got, the more I heard them talking, so I slowed my stride.

"You're awful happy to be here, I didn't think you'd show up after our lunch date," Chyna said. "Hey Kez, come and meet my brother. Kez, Hope. Hope, Kez," Chyna called out to me as I approached and introduced us.

"Sup!" I tilted my head up and stared him down to see if I felt anything off about him.

"What's up man, I've heard so many good things about you. Sissy holds you up there with God, my nigga," he reached in to shake my hand. This nigga was happier than a baby in a barrel full of titties. He couldn't be the fuck nigga that busted me in the head. If it was, he had to be the greatest actor in the world. Nigga needed an Academy Award.

Shaking his outstretched hand, I felt no reserves. "Nice to meet cha, ya heard me," I half-grinned. "Say Jap bruh, I'm bout to step outside to eat some clouds, feel me." After letting him know I was going to blow a blunt of the sticky shit, I turned to walk away.

Before I was out of earshot, I heard some interesting shit that made me stop at the end of bar to ear hustle.

"Sissy, what did you mean by you didn't think I would come?" Hope questioned, as lost as a blind kid in a forest.

"Judging by the encounter we had today, I just assumed you wouldn't show," Chy returned.

"Earlier?" Hope queried, bemused.

166

"Were you high or something, or are you high now? We met at Pascal's earlier. Remember, I gave you the invite to the party," Chyna countered back just as confused.

"Nah, sissy, I didn't meet anyone but a customer service representative today." Hope responded.

"How did you know to come here tonight, if that's the case?" Jap fact checked Hope.

"I found the invite in the armrest and twin said Pappi gave it to him. I don't know what you talm bout."

Chyna looked utterly confused.

"If you wasn't pregnant, I'd ask you if you were high or drunk as we speak," he said looking at Jap. That nigga looked like he was caught up and wasn't gonna lie for Chy.

"Y'all niggas a lil' old to be playing which twin, huh?" Jap asked as I re-approached the group. I know my brother, and had I not stepped in, he may have lost his license fucking with titty-boy.

"Say bruh, on God, I was at AT&T all day today. I lost my phone day before yesterday. They was on some good bullshit about being backed up on shipping. I spent the day with them to get a new phone," I witnessed Jap's face morphing into the nigga that slapped J-Blues silly. I prayed lil' one could take a beating because it was about to go down.

"Hope, I don't understand." Chyna stated confused. "How did you lose your phone day before yesterday, when you sent me a text to meet you at Pascal's, just yesterday?" Chy questioned and showed him the message thread.

"Sis, I think y'all should take this to your office, they got too many nosey muthafuckas out ya. Ya heard me." Noticing the crowd gathering around, I had to save face for my sis and bro. Bitches be ready to go put everything on *World Star* and *YouTube*. It's like they have a shortcut on their phone or some shit.

After the three of them made their way upstairs and I went to blow, I came back in and chopped it up with my niggas, Fatts and Kink.

"Big Foolie, I see you been fucking with Z tough lately," Fatts smiled and sipped on his glass of dark liquor. Looking over at Kink, he had his usual bottle of Ace. It seemed as if these niggas wanted answers.

I looked around and noticed Zy shooting the shit at a table with Toy and Casey. They seemed to have attached to her like a moth to a flame.

"She's different from the hoes I'm used to, ya heard me, my nigga," I felt myself smiling, and a nigga didn't smile.

"We know, shit yo' ass was all about fucking a bitch and sending her ass back to her husband. Ahhhhh!" Kink reminded me.

"Speaking of which, that crazy ass bitch Faye followed me last week," I told them, gossiping like some hoes.

"Noooo huh?" both Fatts and Kink said in unison. I swore these niggas was long-lost twins instead of first cousins that just met.

"Yeah, son. She showed up in the male bat'rum at the restaurant I took Zy to, asking me to suck my dick and shit. I had just pissed all over the floor." Those niggas turned their noses up like it was the most outrageous thing they had ever heard. I understood though, I wasn't into the R. Kelly shit and neither were they.

"Big Foolie, what the fuck you did to that lady, bruh? You got that dickso gold, huh? Y'all get it, like disco gold, but Dickso gold... Ahhhhh!" Fatts laughed at his own corny ass joke.

I looked at that nigga crazy as hell cuz that shit was lame. "Anyways man, I fell asleep at Zyyah's pad and when I went to leave a nigga had to get AAA to come out. Nigga had three flats, she keyed Pearl, and left a note," I told them as their eyes grew big. Everyone knew how I felt about Pearl, she was my main bitch.

"Say Big Foolie, what the fuck did the note say?" Fatts asked and balled his fist in anger as if it was his Tahoe, known to us as My Hoe.

"She was on some rah, rah shit. Talm bout, she not just gonna lose me to a fat bitch and how she knows her every move and she will hurt her if she has to," I mentioned.

"How the fuck you lose something you never had? Ain't the bitch married to a travel agent or some shit?" Fatts questioned.

"Right and yep. I don't know what the fuck she trippin' on," I looked to both of my lil' dudes.

"What you gonna do, Big Dawg?" Kink asked as his eyes almost protruded from his head.

"What are you going to do about what?" Zyyah asked as she rubbed her hands down my chest. She was feeling herself. She knew what the fuck she was doing, yeah.

"You better stop playing with a nigga in here, girl. You know what it's hitting fa," I warned as I pulled her onto my lap. Surprisingly she met me with a kiss.

"I think I'm drunk, baby. I don't want to ruin the rest of your night so, I will hail a cab or an Uber home, ok," she pulled her phone out to call a ride. "You're so freaking cute and sexy," she barely got out before she kissed me again.

Looking toward my lil' homies, they watched in amusement. I assumed they looked that way because they had never seen me interact with a female. It was new to me too, shit. As mentioned, I was used to fucking the dog shit outta bitches in five-star hotels and sending them hoes back home to their husbands.

"Babe, don't insult my manhood. Put cho phone back in ya purse, ya heard me. Fellas, I'mma take Zy home, we gone get up later today on the blacktop since we missed Wednesday," I dapped them up.

Just as we stood to leave Miguel's *Adorn* blared through the speakers.

Yeah, These lips, can't wait to taste your skin, baby,
No, No. And these eyes, yeah, can't wait to see your grin,
Ooh baby. Just let my love, just let my love adorn you,
Please, baby yeah. And you gotta know, know that I
adore...

Zyyah belted out with her hands in the air. The look on everyone's face showed shock, leaving me to feel like I had won. My baby had the voice of seraphim. She sat down in the chair that I was sitting in and finished the song.

"That is my stuff, I love Miguel," she smiled.

"After that rendition, I love Miguel too. Why you not signed, chick?" LaToy questioned. The look in Zy's eyes told me that, that particular question had hit her hard. After our talk the other night, I understood that look to mean 'get me out of here'.

"Aight then folks, we out. Let's go, bae." Extending my hand, I helped her to her feet.

With that, we headed to my car, I drove the hooptie tonight. As soon as I closed her door, my phone rang. Who else was it besides the crazy ass bitch Faye. I hit ignore on that hoe. Immediately, I received a text.

CP: Meet me at the Motel on the side of the overpass in Gentilly, headed to the east.

Message received: 1:55 a.m.

Me: Since when we met at Motels? Your husband finally got smart n cut ya dumass off huh bitch?

Message read: 1:56 a.m.

CP: I got 10k to invest in that dick, so come fuck me one last time.

Message received: 1:58 a.m

"Man, I can't believe this muthafucka would stoop so low to pretend to be me, to ruin my relationship with our own sissy. This nigga on some fuck shit, he think I whooped his ass last time. Oooooh. Just wait til I catch up with his fuck ass!" Hope scolded himself aloud as he walked past me.

Ignoring the lil' tantrum Hope was having, I contemplated whether or not I should go dick this hoe down and get this money. I knew that her moms was in Hospice and she was the lead Cardiologist at University Hospital. *Maybe she kicked the bucket and left ol' girl some money,* I thought to myself.

"Jacques. Babeeeeee. I need to gooooooo!" I looked over my shoulder and noticed Zy had gotten out of the car and was standing there looking at me. I don't know how long she had been standing there, but she didn't seem slighted, just pressed to get home. Rightfully so, she was lit as a muthafucka.

"Get in the car, Zy. We finna go, bae. Let me take care of this lil' situation." After she closed her door, I responded.

Me: I will meet you Saturday at 11:30 p.m. at the Roosevelt Hotel. Book the room and send me the info bitch.

Message read: 2:00 a.m.

CP: Do you really have to be so disrespectful tho, see you next week bae. (kissy face emoji)

Message received: 2:02 a.m.

Following the text message, I got into the driver's seat and looked over at the woman who was slowly stealing my heart. It had barely been a few months, but the more time I spent with her, the more she broke the chains that surrounded my main organ. She slept like a tired child all the way to her apartment.

"Baby, we here," I spoke through her light snores. "Babe, wake up." With a little more urgency in my voice, I spoke louder, and her eyes fluttered open.

A smile danced across her lips. "You're so stinking cute, you know that," she slurred.

I thought it was cool that she was finally admitting that a nigga looked good, but I didn't like that she had to get drunk to do it. Regardless, I smiled at her with lust-filled eyes because she was sexy as fuck. She made me feel like *Lotus Flower Bomb* round this bitch. When I was low she took me high, and I wanted to teach her all the sounds of love.

"Baby, I'mma walk you to your door ok."

I felt like someone was lurking and I would never put her in harm's way. Getting out of the car, I walked around to her side and opened the door. Holding her around her waist, I had my free hand on my pistol. That bitch Faye was a nutcase and I wasn't taking no chances. If she popped out the bushes on some shit, I was gone burn her ass.

As we got to the door, she turned the key and went in, leaving it open. Realizing I wasn't behind her, she turned and beckoned for me with her finger. I looked around and pointed at myself. She smiled and nodded her head up and down in a 'yes' manner. Crossing the threshold, I kicked my shoes off, locked the door, and followed her to the forbidden area of her apartment.

By the time I made it to her room, she had already stripped her shirt off. Exposing her beautiful DD breast that wasn't covered, she sat on the light blue tufted storage bench at the foot of her bed. It set her room off with the navy and cream decorated bedspread and pictures around her walls. Her room was like a safe haven. Holding her left leg up in the air, she asked me to remove her boot and I obliged, immediately removing the other.

She stood and removed her fitted jeans. Damn she was sexy as fuck. I didn't expect her to be as toned as she was. Not saying that I thought she was fat, but I expected her to have a little more flab in the middle. I was happy she didn't trick a nigga with Spanx like a lot of hoes did. "Take a picture, it would last longer," she slurred and laughed.

"What you talm bout, girl. Shiid, a nigga will never forget this visual," I replied and licked my lips.

"I'mma go take a shower, make yourself comfortable."

Tonight is the night that you make me a woman,
you said you'd be gentle with me,
and I hope you will...

She sang to me as she stood in the doorway and removed her barely there G-string. *Damn, my boo is fine as fuck. I'm bout to blow that fuckin back out,* I thought, as I eyed the happy trail that led its way to her juice box.

While she showered, I made my way to the hall bathroom and washed up. A nigga wasn't into that trifling shit, ya heard me. I made it back just as she crawled into bed. Her ass was tooted up in the air. Damn, her box was beautiful and plump as it peaked through the safety of her thick thighs. Walking right up behind her, I smacked her ass and she made her cheeks smack together like a stripper.

"Oh shit girl, you wanna tell a nigga something?" I questioned as my manhood immediately stood at attention.

"Yes, daddy. I need that good wood in my life. It's been four years, five months, and twenty-six days," she slurred. Turning over on her back, she spread eagle. That pussy looked even better after knowing it ain't been touched in almost four and a half years. I rubbed her pussy with my middle and ring fingers and that shit felt like heaven on earth. It was so wet, I tried to slide my thick middle finger into the spot, but the tightness of the tiny hole resisted. *Damn this is gone be amazing, like breaking a virgin,* I thought as my dick hardened, that much more.

"Ooooh, Jacques. Come here, daddy," she said as she pulled me into her and sucked her juices off of my fingers. That shit was sexy as fuck. I been with some freaks, but that shit was on a whole different level. That shit was major leagues. She kissed me so passionately, I couldn't taste shit but toothpaste and liquor. As bad as I wanted to make love to this woman, I couldn't.

"Baby, I can't do this." Surprising myself, I spit it out while still grinding my hips on top of her.

"You what?" she whispered.

"I can't have sex with you," I repeated. "As bad as I want to eat that pussy up and beat that pussy up, I can't consciously do it with you in this state of mind. I want this to be a special moment between us. I want you to remember every touch, every smell, every sound." As I finished my statement, a tear escaped her eye.

"Baby, don't cry," I kissed her tears, then her lips. "C'mere, baby. I don't want you to wake up in the morning and regret having sex with me. I want you to be sober when we take this step."

I moved up to the pillows and pulled her, so she could join me. Facing each other, we kissed more, and I sucked her titties, unable to resist the perkiness that teased at me. She moaned sexy as a muthafucka further turning me on. I had to stop and just hold her. Before long, we both climbed under her blanket and had fallen to sleep.

Chapter 21 - Hope

It had been four days since me and Faith had a falling out over that fuck shit he pulled with Chyna. I couldn't believe he was that spiteful. Nigga acted like the Labrinth song, *Jealous* for no fuckin reason. I had no intention of dropping him for Chyna, I just wanted to form a bond with her, too. He knew how I felt about family. If I hadn't have found the invite that he carelessly left in my car, I wouldn't have known anything about how he mistreated her, while posing as me. Funny thing me and sissy had in common was that we paid attention to minor details.

When she told me how he acted with her, I was livid. Every time he said something that was off, she remembered my responses to her, by voice and in text. Such as sis vs. Sissy, I called her big sissy and he kept calling her sis. We discussed her being pregnant in detail from her nerves to the following excitement. He said he didn't recall her telling him that she was pregnant. I don't know what he thought was going to happen, but God works in mysterious ways. Thinking back, I remember the busted look he had on his face when I walked in asking him about the invitation.

"Ion know what the fuck you holding a grudge against me for. That bitch don't give a fuck about neither one of us," Faith interrupted my thoughts. "I was doing your fuck ass a favor, with your willy-nilly ass. You swear everybody love you like you love them. Ha, ha, ha," he laughed, further pissing me off.

I got up to leave before he made me fuck him up, on some real shit. As I headed towards the door he was still bumping his gums. He kept trying me and I was doing my best to ignore him.

"I'm going to reign terror on them fuck boys and I don't give a fuck who get caught in the crossfire."

"I'm only gonna say this once Twin, if you hurt big sissy again, you gone have to see me, my nigga," I scowled. I was ready to jump on his ass right then.

"Nigga, you already choosing sides. Look at you, we was in the womb together. You barely knew this bitch a month and you already wanna fight me for that hoe," he replied in a pissed manner.

Placing my hand on the doorknob to exit, "Who said anything about fighting?" I smirked and walked out.

"The fuck that mean, Big Twin? You threatening me?" he question immediately after he swung the door open and I made it to my whip. I winked my eye at him, got into the driver's seat, and went on about my way.

Pulling up to Drago's, I got out and headed in. I had promised big sissy to make up to her for what Faith had done. I wasn't a fan of seafood which she was now aware of, however, I heard that the boneless short ribs there were the bidness.

Walking in, I noticed sissy sitting in a corner table alone eating a taco. *Look at her lil' hungry ass, couldn't even wait on a nigga,* I thought. A smile danced across my eyes just from the feeling of having a second chance. In route, I came in contact with a very familiar face. I couldn't remember from where, so I kept it moving.

"Hey, don't I know you?" a soft voice said as she grabbed my arm.

Looking down at her hand like it was the plague, she snatched it back and immediately apologized. "Nah, no apology necessary. I just don't like strangers grabbing on me," I guess sissy saw the commotion and came up to where we stood.

"Lil' bro, you good?" she said as if she was bout that life.

"Chyna-Sinc?" the girl asked. "It's me, D'Asia, your recovery nurse. Nice to see you, suge," she smiled, causing Chyna to seemingly lighten up.

"Oh, girl, I just saw distress on my lil' brother's face and I was on my way to put in work. You know how it is, family values," Sissy said, never breaking eye contact.

"Do I ever, I am a child of six, and I don't play behind none of my siblings, especially my twin with his crazy ass." They laughed.

I knew my memory served me correctly, she was definitely familiar. It was the chick with love on her brain at the hospital. "Sissy, I'm good. Let me holla at Miss D'Asia for a minute, you and the unborn can get back to whatever y'all was eating." Playfully rolling her twinkled eyes, she headed in the direction of the table that held her appetizer.

"What's good with you? I wanted to holla at you at the hospital, but I didn't want to seem thirsty," D'Asia spoke, breaking the awkward silence.

"So you just go around hollering at niggas, huh?" I responded while holding back a smile.

"Nah, not any nigga, just the one I'm interested in."

"Ok, I see you, lil' mama. Go-getter huh, I can respect that."

"Closed mouths don't get fed and I'm hungry for my king out here," I could tell that she was an intelligent hood chick. She had swagger and intellect, just like I liked my girls.

"Let me get ya number, boo. I'm kinda on a date with my sissy. We can link up and get to know each other another time," I smiled and apologized with my eyes.

"Where's your phone, silly? Or do you want me to write it on this napkin?" she laughed as I gave her my phone. I sent her a text, so she could lock me in, then headed in Chyna's direction.

"So what's up, sissy?" I asked as I took my seat at the table.

"Nothing much, can't stop stuffing my face. This baby is going to put some weight on me. After all the years I have been fighting to keep it off, Ghi would have a ball at my expense." Sissy smiled and looked off into the distance as she mentioned the name.

"Ghi, who is that?" I asked nosily.

"Sorry lil' bro, I'm gonna get teary-eyed. Every time I think of my best friend, I do."

"I don't wanna see you cry, big sissy, but I do wanna know why y'all not friends no more."

After staring at me long and hard, a few tears rolled down her cheeks, and I handed her a napkin. "Thank you," she sniffled and wiped her nose. "Long story short, Pappi killed her a little over year ago. Sunday is the anniversary of her funeral."

"Sissy, what you mean Pappi killed her?" I asked confused.

"He shot her and left her for dead," she stated in a simple tone. The way she said it was like she was unattached to the whole ordeal. "Supposedly he thought it was Jap or Kez."

Our donor was dirtier than I thought. I needed to tell her everything so I could clear my conscience. Faith, I could handle. I was afraid of what Pappi would do if he found out...

Chapter 22 – Chyna

After getting to know lil' bro, I was excited, sad, and confused. I wondered why Pappi kept them a secret, it wasn't as if he'd cheated on me or Naomi. I would have loved to know my brothers all of their lives. It had been revealed to me that Faith didn't want anything to do with me because of Pappi's choice to keep them a secret. I wished he wouldn't hold a grudge against me for something so trivial, it wasn't as if I had a choice in any of it.

Had I listened to Ju'an and not given Hope another shot, I wouldn't have known that he and Faith were sent at them by Pappi. It pissed me off that I was caught up in a crossfire. First my best friend dies, then I get shot and could've potentially lost my child. What did he have planned next? As I sat on the side of Ju'an's bed in deep thought, he exited the bathroom in a nice blue robe. All I could do was think of disrobing him. I couldn't wait to have this baby. All I did since I've been pregnant was eat and have sex. Have sex and eat.

"Why you looking at me with the 'come fuck me' eyes, Fatt?" Ju'an referred to me by a name he gave me some time ago. "You want some of this, don't you?" Allowing his robe to flap open, I started to salivate at his beautiful member. It was a tad darker than his body so it stood out from his canvass .

"Is that all you think about? Sex, sex, sex?" I questioned while thinking of how deep that dick could've been up in me.

"You know you want this, don't play," he licked his lips. That simple gesture made me want to suck his dick instantly. I had been so damn horny, I hoped I was carrying a boy.

Bzz. Bzz. Bzz. Jap's phone buzzed alerting him of a text. He quickly walked over and grabbed his phone. Whatever the message was, made him smile and I was kind of snubbed. What the fuck was coming to his phone this time of night to cause that kind of smile? I was sitting right here.

Noticing the scowl my face held, he walked over to me and grabbed my cheeks to face him. "I finally got the information I've been waiting on. This bullshit is about to be laid to rest, baby. We're gonna be able to step outside without having to look over our shoulders anymore," the smile on his face told me he was relieved as much as he was up to no good.

"What are you about to do, Ju'an?" I questioned.

"The less you know, the better. Now, take them panties off," he commanded.

"Not this time, you will not sex me into submission. Plus, I have something I need to tell you. I have been afraid to tell you this, but I think it's time you know." My voice was shaky but serious.

"Chyna, you got my nerves bad. Go on and spit that shit out," he said as I watched the love and friendliness leave his face. It was like he automatically thought the worst.

I took a deep breath and looked in his direction. I felt myself hyperventilating, it was like all of the air was escaping the room and I could no longer breathe or talk.

"Chyna, what's the deal? What got you so pressed that you aren't able to say what you need to say, man? I know you better not be on no fuck shit."

"What you mean by fuck shit, Ju'an?" I defended.

"C'mon man, don't try to turn the tables. I hate when you do that. Tell me what you know that was so bad that you had to 'find the right time' to tell me," he air quoted.

"I don't wanna argue, so here it is. Hope told me that him and Faith was sent at y'all by Pappi. He was so afraid to tell me that he cried and begged me not to say anything. He felt the need to warn me because we talked about Ghi. It was his belief that if Pappi would take my best friend out after knowing her all of her life, he would have no problem taking you and Kez out. Regardless of you being my child's father and Kez being so close to my heart. I questioned him as to why he would sell himself and his twin out," I began to wonder if he was a mole sent by Pappi. The little fish that distracted the big fish while the shark ate them both.

"Well?"

"Well what?" I asked obliviously.

"Why is he willing to come forth with this information now? I told you I didn't trust them niggas. I'm just not the type of dude to stand between familial relationships, that's why I didn't press the issue," Ju'an said and I wanted to argue, but I couldn't. I had been a bad judge of character, blinded by ancestral love, love of family and bonding.

"Well, supposedly he wanted nothing to do with any of the things that had been popping off. The night I got shot, he said that Pappi had told them nothing of our involvement, nor did he say who you guys were. It was supposedly the last time he would ask them to handle any of his street business. He was under the impression that they were settling a score between Pappi and some niggas that robbed him. They didn't even know I existed at that point, Hope was the driver and Faith was the howling shooter."

"Chy, can you honestly look me in the face and tell me you believe every word he told you?"

"Baby, you had to be there to understand. He actually wanted to talk to you, but knowing your temper, I warned him against it," I stated absentmindedly. "Ju'an, he is just a hood boy that doesn't want to be of the environment, because he is from the environment. He is tired of living in his younger brother's shadow. All he wants is a college education and a better life. Pappi promised him a full ride once they took care of this last hit, but he can't go through with it now, knowing who we are."

"Chyna, I know you hear what you're saying, but are you listening? Does any of what you're saying to me, make sense to you? Why is he throwing them under the bus now? What's in it for him?" He looked at me in a state of wonder. *Had I lost my mind?* I thought.

Replaying the scene at the restaurant, I couldn't imagine that he was a swindler. My lack of street knowledge had me second-guessing my own judgment. With Naomi trying to rob me and Pappi trying to kill the father of my child, and the only people who loved me, I just didn't know anymore.

"I need a vacation," I said in an exasperated tone. Tears rolled down my face by the bucketloads because of my uncertainty and lack of knowledge of dirty ass people.

"I know baby, I know. Don't cry though, it'll all be over soon. Book a flight and a hotel in Dubai for the week of Valentine's. See if Kez and Fatts wanna go, too. Make this a family thing," he kissed my forehead and held me tightly until I fell asleep.

$$$$

Waking up on a Sunday to Ju'an not being in his own bed or in his mancave, had thrown me for a loop. After making my rounds to check for him, I showered and threw on one of his oversized collegiate t-shirts. Sure, I had clothes at his house, but I wanted to be comfortable. Truthfully, I wanted to be naked but didn't want to run the risk of him returning with someone and being exposed. After lathering myself down with *Tatcha Indigo Cream* from Sephora, I headed to the kitchen to feed my face.

No sooner than I had finished my breakfast, cleaned up my mess, and walked into the back of the house, Ju'an entered with Fatts and Kink. Anyone who didn't know the two of them, would've never known that they weren't brothers.

"So Foolie, you got a whole damn private investigator?" Fatts questioned.

"Nah, I got a whole damn tracker on both of their whips, my dude. I'm doing my own private investigation. I'm not gonna risk our lives or Chyna and my unborn. I'm not leaving our fate in the hands of a psycho and his spawns," Ju'an said. He was so protective of me. It was both noble and necessary, with everything that my parents were capable of. I loved that man with every fiber of my being.

I heard his footsteps coming down the hallway. Immediately, I threw my earbuds in and pretended to be listening to an audiobook with my back turned. "Baby," he called out and I ignored him.

Deciding to shake the bed since he assumed that I didn't hear him, I jumped as if I had been startled. I turned to him and smiled. "You scared me, baby."

"I told that ass about having both earbuds in. With everything that's happening, I need you to be on alert, Chy," he scolded.

"Hope called me while you were out. He's leaving for Tucson, Arizona soon so he can get settled in before starting at University of Arizona." Happy for lil' bro, I could only hope no one threw a wrench in his dream of becoming a lawyer.

Rat tat, tat, tat, tat. The sound of a machine gun and glass breaking in the front of the house had me frozen in time...

Chapter 23 – Fatts

"What the fuck man! Kink! Kink! You good cuz? Kink?" I yelled, crawling over to my cousin who was covered in blood. Once I got to him, he was staring into space. I shook him to see if he was dead or alive. Finally, he blinked his eyes and I let the breath go that I was unknowingly holding.

He sat up as Jap ran into the living room with his heat in his hand.

"Bruh, what the fuck. How you tracking a nigga and don't know he in front ya damn house, Foolie?" I asked, still checking for my cousin.

I knew it had to be them because Jap didn't have enemies. He pulled his phone out and opened up an app as he sat next to us on the floor checking Kink.

"It was the green Cut dog that was in this area last," he spoke to himself more than me. "U of A my ass, that nigga is dead meat." Running to the back of the house, I heard him yelling at big sis. Truthfully, that had pissed me off, but I had to find out where all of the blood was coming from that kept oozing down the side of Kink's face.

"My fuckin head feel like I got a lot of pressure building up," Kink said.

"I gotta get you to the hospital, my nigga," I informed him but didn't tell him why, not wanting him to freak the fuck out about the big piece of vase sticking out the side of his head.

He raised his hand to feel the area, but I warned him against it. "Yo, Big Foolie, I'mma need you to come take us to the ER, my boy."

"Oh my God Kink, you got a big ass pie—" Chyna stopped when she realized my eyes were pleading with her to not say another word. Getting cousin to his feet, we headed to the door.

When we made it outside, Jap's car sat on three flats. I could tell he was livid, but he refused to allow us to see him under pressure. "Let's just take your car babe, he needs to get to the hospital," he said to Chyna who looked like she didn't want the blood all over her interior.

Hitting the alarm on the key fob, we headed to her car and noticed her shit was on flats, too. She still had just a t-shirt on but I had to get cuz to the hospital, I didn't have time for all that changing. I didn't say shit about it.

I was trying to avoid getting into my truck because it sat so high off of the ground. It was our last resort, plus it looked like the only safe bet since there were no obvious damages. Opening the back door, we let Kink and Chy in from the passenger side. Jap got in the front passenger seat and I walked around to drive. Immediately, I knew that bitch nigga had to DIE!

There was a knife in each tire on the driver's side, 'U Nex Bitch Boi,' was spray painted in huge letters, and my tail light wires were routed into the gas tank... that nigga tried to take the kid out.

"Big sis, I know them lil' niggas is your brothers, but they gotta die. They signed their death certificates when they fucked with My Hoe," I was fuming as I yelled inside of the truck towards the back seat where Chyna sat with Kink.

"I can't blame you, my dude. However, I need you to focus on the matter at hand. That's getting Kink to the hospital like, twenty minutes ago. He's losing a lot of blood, bro," Jap attempted to calm me down.

"Guys, guys, whatever it is that y'all are going to do, ya best do it now! I think we might be losing him..."

$$$$

One stolen whip and three hours later, I had to call Kink's mom and pops to let them know that he was in the hospital. Thank God for my skills, if we would've had to wait for a fuck ass ambulance, my cousin would be dead. It didn't matter which neighborhood you lived in anymore, them bitches picked and chose severity by name and dialect of English.

"Ayyyye, what happen, ya heard me?" Kez walked into the waiting area and dapped us up.

"Fuck boys hunted the hunter. Kink was a casualty of war. We are waiting on the surgeon to come out," I replied salty as fuck.

"Lil' bro, you wanna get something off ya chest, my dude?" Jap questioned like I was some hoe ass nigga.

"Say, Big Foolie, a nigga ain't being disrespectful or nothing, bruh. I definitely ain't blaming you for what happened because we dealing with some slick ass snakes. If I said that I ain't pissed the fuck off though, I would be lying for real, for real."

"Family of Kinrick Hawkins," a petite white, doctor called out.

"Yeah, we right here, ya heard me," Kez responded while me and Jap had a standoff.

"Kinrick will live, he will make a full recovery. He is stitched up and his head is swollen due to the traumatic injury. Thank goodness it was more of a superficial cut, that was why he lost so much blood," she informed us.

Chyna hugged me and rubbed my back. As she did that, I stared at Jap, thinking my nigga was blessed my cousin didn't die. I still didn't understand how the fuck he was investigating these fools and didn't know that they were right outside of his house. We hadn't been inside thirty minutes before everything popped off.

"Where them niggas at right now? I wanna apologize to you now, big sis. The next time we cross paths, they gone be in the morgue."

Chapter 24 – Jacques

It had been a week since the Christmas party and I was getting more and more attached to the woman that saved my life months ago. She was everything a nigga never thought he needed. Never in a million years, had I seen myself with one woman after being scorned by a pissy pussy bitch in middle school.

"Where are you taking me, Jacques? We've been driving for like two hours?" Zy smiled and looked towards me from the passenger seat of the rental car.

"Look woman, can you just enjoy the scenery and let me surprise you for a change?"

"Yes I can, but my butt is getting numb, you heard me?" she asked, making a mockery of the natives' slang. It was hilarious to me because it was prim and proper, in her typical Arizona-English dialect. "We've left Louisiana, driven through Mississippi, now I see a 'Welcome to Alabama' sign. Can I at least have a clue?"

"Yep, you're going to love it. Give daddy a kiss," I replied with a smirk. I knew she would love where I was taking her, because she was a simple woman. For that reason alone, I felt like she deserved the world and I was going to give it to her.

"Well, since you told me not to pack a bag or get dolled up, I hope it's somewhere casual," she responded. "Do you mind if I finish reading this book since it seems like we are going to New York, or did you wanna talk?"

"Say bruh, you silly, yeah. You know you didn't have to ask to read your book, girl. But what you reading, though?" I asked nosily. Another quality of mine that caught her by surprise, I loved to read. Especially a good urban book.

"I'm almost finished with *Lovin A Young Rich Savage 2*, by Evelyn Latrice." We finished the author's name in unison, causing her to look at me weird. "Now what do you know about her?" Z queried.

"I know that she is a great storyteller and I know that Choice and Chance was my muthafuckas. I would've had to put hands on Hyra though. We probably wouldn't have made it. Her story explained her attitude, so in the end I understood. We got about forty-five minutes to our hotel. What chapter you on, bae?" I asked. Them boys reminded me of me and Jap.

"I'm at the part where Elisha had to smoke a blunt to calm her nerves in the studio. Ha, ha," she laughed.

"What's so funny?"

"Nothing really. I just read the lyrics to the song she was singing, and it made me think about where this thing with us was going." Zy turned off her Kindle and faced me.

"Where do *you* see it going, Z?" Placing the ball in her court, I wanted to know what she saw in our future.

With her eyes smiling from her cheeks, she stared at the roof of the Tahoe I had rented for our two-day vacation. It was as if she searched it for her response. "I just want us both to be happy, not feel rushed into anything, and to explore and enjoy getting to know one another."

"So you want to be friends, is what you saying?" I clarified.

"I hope you don't think I'm stringing you along, and I pray that you don't think I am pinning my past transgressions on you. I just want us to be comfortable with each other before we put titles on anything. Ya heard me?" she smiled. Her aura was intoxicating.

"I can dig it, lil' mama. You just getting to the good part. We got about thirty minutes left, so gone get finished so we can leave Evelyn Shields a review." She looked at me crazy.

"Her name isn't Evelyn Shields, it's definitely Evelyn Latrice," she looked at the Kindle to confirm.

"Oh but it's definitely Evelyn Shields, boo-boo. I been following her career since day one, back when Block Boyz was Beauty and the Block. Don't come at me sideways because I rather have you come at me straight, ok? Ok!" I tried my best to sound like a female but failed, miserably. We both laughed, leaving Z to turn her Kindle back on to finish her read.

$$$$

Looking over at my baby who had fallen asleep, after or in the middle of her read, we had pulled into the lot of the Hampton Inn, Gulf Shores, AL. "Zy, baby wake up," I called to her and she opened her eyes.

"OMG, this is beautiful! Where are we?" she asked. "It looks like something I Googled on the internet."

"We have arrived at our destination. I am Jacques and I will be your travel guide today. Hold tight and I will be over to open your door so that we may start our tour of Gulf Shores, Alabama. We'll be staying at the beautiful Hampton Inn, which offers a double King room. There are two King beds, a television, a desk, a full bath, and a great view. Also offered, is free Wi-Fi and a complimentary breakfast bar, in which we may or may not use depending on the activities of the night," I winked, which caused her to smile.

"I would have never taken you for the guy that you are at your core. With the rough exterior you have, you amaze me more and more," she complimented as she kissed my jaw.

She grabbed her handbag and I held my hand out so that she could hold onto me, her knight in shining armor, as she stepped down. "Let's go get checked in so we can get settled and start our vacation. First up, shopping," I wiggled my eyebrows suggestively.

Grabbing the room key from the front desk lady, we headed to the elevators. As we entered and stood near the back, I couldn't help but notice the excitement in Zyyah's eyes. "I truly hope you enjoy everything that I got planned. Typically, we would come here during the spring or summer for the water activities. With everything that been popping off lately, I figured we could both use the escape."

"I'm glad I was your woman of choice for your mental health break from the hustle and bustle of the city life," she said her soft hand into mine.

We exited to the left and made it to our room. Sliding the key card, I allowed Zy to enter first. Walking up to the bed she stopped, and her mouth dropped. There laid an after five dress for her and a tuxedo for me, with a cummerbund and bowtie the same color as her dress.

"What is this?" she asked excitedly.

"One of my homeboys is having a gala to raise money for abused and neglected children. I figured we would go, but we don't have to go if you don't want to."

"Are you crazy? I would love to go. This is a major milestone for him and the kids and I am pretty sure the tickets were pretty pricy. You are trying to break my protective walls down at every turn, aren't you?"

"I was hoping you wanted to go, ya heard me. I got these tickets and this whole lil' get up after the Christmas party. We gotta go get shoes and whatever else you will need, to get all dolled up and do the lil' girly shit y'all do. But first things first, food, cuz a nigga is starving."

"How did you know what size dress to get?" Zy asked.

"Look, don't worry about all that. I just know, ok. Now let's go cuz a nigga need to eat. The event starts at eight, it's barely eleven."

$$$$

I walked up behind Zy sitting at the vanity spraying something on her face. When she opened her eyes, all I could do was take in her beauty. I had been doing that a lot lately. I had to question my thug. The woman before me was changing me. My thoughts, my actions, even my speech was slowly being altered.

"Why are you staring? Haven't your mother ever told you it was rude to stare, if you take a picture, it would last longer." She smiled modestly.

All I could do was stand there and bite my lip, before I was forced to strip her down to her birthday suit and have my mufuckin way with her fine ass.

"You look good, bae! When we walk in the place it's gone be like the Tupac song, *All Eyes On Us*." Finally able to speak, that was the best I could do. Lame as fuck.

"What time are we leaving?" she asked as she sprayed her perfume in the air and did a walk through. I was intrigued. "What? I don't want my fragrance to be overpowering."

"Shiiiid, the way that dress hugging them curves, I don't think I wanna go." She looked at me with wide eyes. "On the real, a nigga just wanna cum," I rolled my hips and bit my lip, with lust in my eyes.

"You are so freaking silly, boy. We have all weekend for that," she said and kissed my lips.

"Don't play with a nigga feelings bruh, for real," I looked at her with a serious face.

"Boy, let's go. You are taking up too much time. Where is the gala?"

"Oh, it's in the Conference room downstairs. Let's go!"

Grabbing her hand, we headed out to support my dawg. We all came from rough backgrounds. Once he made it, he said no more kids would suffer through hungry nights on his watch. *Three hours later...*

"Oh my God, that was the greatest charity event I've ever been to? Monica Brown... Really? Singing *Greatest Love of All* was the best performance of the night," Zyyah boasted as we entered the room.

She kicked her shoes off at the door, grabbed her silk scarf from the foot of the bed, and tied her hair up. Walking over to the vanity, she pulled out a pack of wipes, sat down, and removed the very light makeup that she wore. I got undressed and took a shower because all of the mingling had me beat.

After showering I donned a pair of grey Polo boxers and a white t-shirt. "Which bed you want bae?" I asked assuming she may have wanted to sleep in her own bed. She had stripped down to her underwear by the time I came out.

"It doesn't matter to me, whichever." Her face still showed excitement and happiness. I could tell that she genuinely enjoyed the event. After she headed into the bat'rum, I jumped into the bed that had all of her bags and stuff on it from our shopping trip. I was that nigga.

Chapter 25 – Zyyah

Today was the best day of my life. I had no idea Jacques knew all of these big industry names. His dawg, as he called him, was Lloyd the singer. Like seriously? I was star-struck around all of those A-list people, while he sat there as cool as a cucumber in the produce section. When Lloyd performed *Tru,* I think everyone in the room felt a piece of his soul, I know I did.

Walking out of the bathroom in my lingerie that I snuck in the bag without Jacques noticing, I was ready to give him the business. I cut the corner and took in his light snores. My boo was tired. I noticed he had climbed in the bed that had all of my crap sprawled over it. I purposely didn't drink tonight so that we could consummate our situationship.

As I walked over to him, to put cover over him, I decided to move the things from the foot of the bed and join him. We had fallen asleep together on a few occasions, but tonight was the night. As I grabbed the last bag, I noticed his semi-erect penis head sticking from the slit in his boxers. Sure, I hadn't had sex in forever and a day, but giving head was like riding a bike. The sight of his beautiful member made my mouth water and my vagina tingle like none other.

I placed the bag onto the other bed and took a deep breath. *You can do this Zy, you like him, and he likes you. You have made him wait long enough, give that man some of the good stuff that he has worked for.* Feeling my nerves getting the best of me, I walked up to the bed and grabbed his thick pole.

I wrapped my manicured fingers around it, barely able to touch fingertips, I stroked him up and down while squeezing him. Taking notice of his beautiful penis, I licked the tip which caused his eyes to spring open.

"Whachu doing, baby?" Jacques managed to get out between gasps.

"Shhhhh! Let me do this, I got you," I responded, teasing his head with circular motions of my tongue. Opening my mouth wide enough, I chased my hand down his pole and bobbed my head while gently massaging him.

"Ooooooooh shit baby, damn. What the fuck you doing to a nigga? Shiiit!" he hissed while grabbing a handful of my hair, just tight enough to let me know that it was good, he loosened his grip.

His nectar was sweet, which made me go harder. I spit on the head and repeated the motion, following my hand up and down his thickness. I felt him get ten times harder as I sucked the soul out of him. Popping him out of my mouth, I looked at him while stroking.

"You like that, daddy?" I questioned.

"Oooh shit baby," was his only response. I licked him from his scrotal sack to his tip and swallowed him again. "Fuuuuuuck. What the fuck you tr—" I didn't allow him to complete his question. I bobbed my head in a quick motion while massaging his scrotum with my hand and caused friction to the main vein with my firm tongue.

"Bring that pussy up here, baby," he requested.

"Ummmmmmmmmm," I hummed on his ball sack while having a hand party with his manhood. "I'm not ready for that part. Let me please you, Jacques," I spoke while eyeing the clear semen oozing. It made me wet as an ocean's floor. Reaching down with my free hand, I played with my vagina.

I let go of his penis, grabbed my boob, and fondled my nipple. "Oooh shit baby, no hands. Got damn girl you a fuckin' bea—" He grabbed his manhood and tried to keep the explosion from escaping down my throat. *Too late.* Goodness, he was sweet, I didn't allow one drop to waste. "Damn girl, come sit on my face."

Finally obliging, I kissed from his hard abs up to his lips. Surprised he embraced the kiss, he nearly swallowed my whole face sloppily. I straddled him, allowing him to feel the heat between my thighs that was onset by his member being in my mouth. I wound my hips in a circular motion, enjoying the feeling of his manhood immediately hardening again.

"Damn girl, you been holding out on a nigga, huh?" he said before grabbing my face and kissing my lips sensually.

He flipped me over, I assumed I was taking too long to straddle his face. Lifting and opening my legs, he kissed each thigh, inch by inch, until he reached my freshly waxed peach. "Damn your pussy is beautiful. Is this your birthmark?" He asked, staring at the discoloration on my left labia majora. Embarrassed, I tried to close my legs. "Um um, baby, what you doing? This pussy was made for me, it's in the shape of a 'K.' This Kez pussy," he said before he kissed my lower lips.

I was quivering before the real deal started. Rubbing my clit with his thumb, he smiled. "Damn, you smell so fuckin' good," he inhaled at the opening of my lips. The warmth of the breath he released, caused me a great feeling of euphoria. He licked my opening from the bottom to the top, latching onto my clit with his teeth. He sucked and licked, causing my valley to give off an unlimited supply of desired wetness. It felt so great that I thought I would sink into the thick mattress and disappear.

After he got me to his height of bliss, he pushed his thick finger through the tightness of my vaginal opening. Eventually getting his finger in as far as he could, he massaged the inside of my girl and the clit with his thumb. It felt like he was trying to rub his fingers together and that was amazing.

"You ready for this dick, bae?" He devoured my coochie like it was a buffet, I didn't think he was ready for *my girl*. I was speechless and in a state of bliss.

Finally, satisfied with the tongue lashing, he kissed from the top of my vagina to my boobs. Paying equal attention to both as he sucked one and fondled the other, he found my lips and took the bottom one into his mouth. We kissed again, more passionately than the first time. "Damn baby, you doing something to a nigga heart. Bruh." Rubbing his penis against the opening, my eyes bucked from my head. I had just taken him down my throat, but, it felt much bigger against the smaller opening of my vagina. "Don't worry, baby. Daddy gone finesse that sweet pussy. I promise I'mma take care of your heart, your mind, and your body. They all belong to me."

He eased the head in, causing pain and pleasure. "Damn baby, this snapper tight as fuck," he breathed into my ear. I grabbed ahold of his back. "Um um, lemme see, bae," he got on his knees and grabbed both thighs at the inner and spread them apart. He guided his huge penis into my hole. I swear it felt like he was breaking my hymen all over again. "Oooh shit baby, this snapback feel so good wrapped around my dick. It's like it was made for me."

"Ahhhhh daddy, get it all in and stop teasing this pussy," the words that escaped my lips in ecstasy caused him to stare at me with a devilish grin.

"Daddy like that shit. Keep talking dirty to me, bae. You gone make me fuck the shit outta you, yeah," I smiled and grabbed my left boob placing the nipple in my mouth. "Fuck girl, what is you doing to a nigga," he pushed in all the way, causing me to yelp out in pleasure.

He laid back down and nibbled my earlobe.

"Ooooh, shit that dick feels so good, baby!" I cooed in his ear and grabbed the back of his head. He pumped in and out of me like he was drilling for oil.

"Damn baby, that snapper is so fuckin good. I can't hold out no longer. I'm about to bust if you don't stop throwing it in a circle on this dick. Grrr!" he growled in my ear and bit down on my lobe, harder. I screamed so loud that I thought I had woken up the whole hotel. We both reached euphoric heights as we orgasmed together. He laid atop of me, in our afterglow as we caught our breaths...

"Bae, you straight?" Jacques questioned as he rolled onto his side and propped himself up on his elbow. The lust was ever-present in his beautiful eyes. He rubbed my naked stomach in a loving manner and I just looked at him.

"I'm wonderful, embarrassed, but wonderful," I admitted with a smile on my face.

"What are you embarrassed for? That pussy was the shit, bae. The fuck?"

"I can't believe I spoke that way. I haven't swore in years," I covered my eyes.

"That's cuz daddy put that dick on ya ass and you loved that shit," he squeezed my boob and smiled. "I'm bout to hit this shower, you coming or you wanna shower by yaself?"

"I already came... a few times! I wanna come in the shower too, so let's go, daddy!" I headed to the bathroom and started our shower.

$$$$

"Good morning baby, I went to the lil' kitchen and grabbed us breakfast. You were sleeping so peacefully, I decided not to wake you." Jacques kissed me on the lips as I exited the bathroom.

"I thought we'd head over to the seafood shack that we passed down on the beach yesterday," I responded.

"Oh yeah baby, that's cool. We can do that. You can have whatever you like, ya heard me," he smiled as we sat at the small dining table that was set midway the picture window.

Jacques' phone kept buzzing. It wasn't the buzzing that annoyed me, it was the fact that he kept ignoring it. "Baby, are you going to get that? It has to be important, whoever it is keeps texting back to back."

"I'll get it when we finish breakfast. I brought you out chere so we could be undisturbed. This fuckin' phone hasn't stopped. These niggas know what it's hitting for. Well not really, but they knew I didn't wanna be disturbed the whole weekend," he stuffed a piece of bacon in his mouth unbothered.

Finishing our breakfast and heading out to walk along the beachfront, his phone actually rang. He stopped what he was doing to answer, which didn't bother me one bit. I'd rather a person answer a call or respond to a text any day. If there wasn't anything to hide, that simple gesture wouldn't be a problem.

"Nah man, that wasn't what was discussed." Frown lines formed in Jacques' forehead, I knew it was trouble in paradise. Immediately, I walked back into the room and started to pack up the things that we had purchased. I was prepared to cut our rendezvous short.

"I'm sorry baby," he mouthed. "Nah, them fuck niggas ain't walking away with that amount of my muthafuckin money. The fuck they think this is?" was the last I heard of the one-sided conversation before he walked out on the balcony, closing the sliding glass door behind him.

It wasn't a bad ride home, I napped the whole way there. I was tired, my baby had stretched me every which way he could've last night into the morning. He was a little nervous when we left, but I didn't want to pry. I mean, I had only had sex with him without strings, I didn't think I was entitled to questions and answers.

Chapter 26 – Jacques/Kez

I don't know who the fuck these fuck niggas think they fuckin' with. Just cuz a nigga been on his calm shit lately, they think they bout to run off on me with fifty stacks? They got the right game, wrong nigga. Closing the back door on the Tahoe, my phone alerted me of a text.

CP: So we taking fat bitches to Gulf Shores now huh?
Message received: 12:16 p.m.

Me: Nah hoe I'm taking beautiful women where they deserve to go.
Message read: 12:17 p.m.

Me: Is you stalking me bitch???
Message read: 12:17 p.m.

CP: Yup now get your ass home before you take a L fuck nigga
Message received: 12:19 p.m.

After reading that last message, I was furious as a muthafucka. I wanted to kill everything moving. Getting into the truck and securing myself, I grabbed a handful of Zyyah's thigh.

"You good baby, you ready to ride?"

"I'm good if you are. I'm tired from the beating you gave me last night, I can't say that I will stay awake on the ride back." Leaning in and kissing my jawbone, she smiled.

"That's cool bae!"

$$$$

"Bae, we here. Wake ya sexy ass up and let's get all of this stuff out. I'm not understanding how we went to three stores and you got so many bags of shit," I called to my sleeping beauty.

"Easy baby, I love fashion. Duh," replying with closed eyes and a smile on her face, she stretched her frame. I exited the whip and grabbed her things. I opened the door for her, even with everything in my hands. It didn't take away the fact that I was feeling some type of way about the woman before me. All I could do from here is pray that she didn't break me. I had had my walls up for so long that I forgot I had a soul. Go hard or go home had been my mentality.

We walked up to her door and a paper was taped on it. Immediately, my heart sank. I just knew that crazy bitch Faye had been over here to threaten her. Grabbing the paper, she looked upset after reading it.

"Everything ok?" I cautioned.

"Yeah, the water in the building will be off until further notice because of a busted pipe. Uggh. I'mma have to pack a bag and get a motel room. There is nothing I can do here without water," she pretended to be ok, but I could tell she was frustrated. "Thank you for a great night, baby. I know you have things to take care of, call me later," she kissed me.

"Shit, I know you better give me a better kiss than that. You got me bent, ya heard me," I knew she was pissed but that shit didn't have anything to do with me. She grabbed my face and gave me a real kiss. "Much better, don't try that shit again." She finally smiled. "Here, I will take care of the hotel bill for you. Don't go to no fuckin motel either, that's for hoes and dope fiends. How often does this shit happen?" I peeled off three one-hundred-dollar bills and handed it to her.

After we talked for a bit, I walked out to my rental and headed in the direction of my drop house. I don't know what the fuck was popping off yesterday, but these niggas got caught up and took a fifty K hit. I'm not finna take that shit sitting down. Pulling into the driveway, I hopped out and went into the house. Niggas sitting in there with naked hoes in they lap, and the living room smoked out.

"What the fuck kind of shit y'all got going on?" I asked causing the two lil' niggas to push the females off they lap.

"Boss, boss, I thought you was out of town til tomorrow," JB said.

"Nigga, I don't pay you to keep tabs on me, I pay you to keep my spot free of hoes that ain't good for nothing but jack moves out chere." No sooner than I said that, a fuck nigga came busting through the back door. I grabbed the naked bitch that was closest to me and used her for a shield as I took aim.

"Please let me go. Don't kill me," she cried. I put my heat to her head.

"Drop ya fuckin pistol my nigga, or baby here is dead!"

"I don't give a fuck, kill that cheating ass bitch. I followed her here after she told me she was going to the mall with this slut!" he said as he pointed his pistol at the other naked bitch. "Hoes haven't been in here fifteen minutes and they both naked," he cried.

"You a broke ass nigga. We chasing the bag bitch, and you chasing a peanut sack. My girl deserves better than you," she laughed in his face and he pulled the trigger, hitting her perfectly between the eyes.

"Noooo. You killed my best friend!"

I let the girl go as she ran up to her boyfriend and slapped him in the face while he stood there in a state of shock. Running to her friend to check on the corpse, the dude turned the gun on himself and pulled the trigger. My spot turned into a blood bath. Because his stupid ass didn't have a silencer we had to clear out the dope and money. What was left of it anyway.

"Meet me at the spot in tree (3), we got shit to discuss," I commanded.

"What about her?" Black asked.

"What about 'er? No witness, no case," I turned to walk to my car.

"No, I promise I won't say anything to five-o," she cried.

Pewt. I sent a bullet crashing through her dome. I knew her response meant if questioned, she would crack under pressure. A nigga didn't have time for that shit.

"Clean this shit up and meet me when the fuck y'all supposed to meet me." On that note, I left.

Bzz, bzz, bzz. My phone vibrated in the cup holder, as I sat waiting on my order from We Never Close. Picking it up, I saw that it was Faye's crazy ass.

CP: you stood me up last night. I got the room for tonight, be there or lose out on this paper. Room 741.

I forgot all about that lil' meeting with her, I was with my boo and I didn't regret a moment of it. I called my guy after receiving the text.

"What up though, meet me at the spot. I need you to handle something, ya heard me," I spoke into my cell.

"Aiight, Big Foolie. Everything good, huh?" Fatts asked. He knew I didn't discuss shit over the airwaves. No telling who was out there trying to intercept keywords and shit.

"Yeah my nigga, it will be in a sec, ya heard me. Leave cuzzo out of this one, feel me?" Was how I responded. It was enough for him to decipher the severity of the situation. Kink was a dope boy, he wasn't a murderer. That was the major difference between him and Fatts.

"I got you. How soon?" he queried.

"Godspeed."

As soon as Fatts showed up, I clued him in on the situation at hand, and we entered the building. Black and JB got there about fifteen minutes ago. Them bitches pissed me off because they sat there shooting the shit and didn't notice me watching them.

"What's good, fellas?" Fatts dapped them up like everything was kosher.

"Waaaan, Wuz hap'n," Black said. He sounded just like the New Orleans rapper B.G.

"Now that the pleasantries are outta da way, either one of y'all mind clueing me in on the L we took yesterday?" I questioned, breaking up the reunion. JB and Black stared at each other.

"What the fuck y'all niggas waiting on? I'm pretty sure he ain't talking to me, my niggas," Fatts probed as he took a seat at the roundtable.

"What happened?" JB stalled. "We thought a nigga was coming for some weight and he came in a robbed us."

"Yeah, what he said," Black backed his cousin.

Taking my phone from my pocket, I placed it on the table and put a slick grin on my face. So slick, it was scary. If them niggas didn't know not to test my gangsta before that moment, they should've learned, or they were about to.

"Y'all wanna try that again? This time, put some respeck on it."

"Boss, a nigga hit us unexpectedly. It was a dude we had been doing business with for a minute, so we didn't think nothing of him wanting a lil' more. Shit, we out chere chasing the bag so we figured that nigga was too," Black spoke that time. I took notice of JB, he had a smirk on his face.

"My lil' niggas, the only thing I hate more than a liar is a thief," I spoke. I dropped the projector screen and hit play on my phone after connecting it to a wire. Seeing that they were being recorded from the time they walked up, to the time they high-fived each other, they got nervous.

"So this dude right here, walked up to the house to score. Y'all dapped up. He entered the pad. Wait right here, Fatts check this out, he bout to have niggas come through the back door to help him rob our spot. Oh, nope no one comes in, he's led to the back by… who is that?"

"JB? Ahhhhhh!" Fatts laughed. I knew that laugh meant he'd be tortured.

"Nigga, y'all even smoked a blunt on the couch after the hit. Must've been some scary ass shit to need to smoke, huh?" They were pouring with sweat. "Now, y'all wanna try this shit again?" I looked at them with a murderous glare.

"Get to fuckin talking, niggas!" Fatts yelled, placing two syringes filled with yellow liquid on the table.

"Well, honestly a nigga was overtaken by greed. I was chasing paper and thought it was a good idea at the time," Black admitted. "JB ain't had shit to do with it. He was against the whole idea."

"Why the fuck you was there if you ain't wanna die, JB?" I was curious. The grown ass nigga sat there and let a tear fall from his eyes.

"Can I call moms one last time and tell her I love her?" was all JB said.

"Don't make me kill her for trying no fuck shit, my nigga," I warned him. "Gone get ya last words out cuz it's lights out for both of y'all." Just as I said that, Black started reaching for something in his Polo boot. Fatts ran over to him and jabbed him in the neck with one of the syringes.

"I was just gonna give my portion of the money back," he handed Fatts an envelope filled with cash and took his last breath.

"I don't have my fifteen, I paid my daughter tuition and took her shopping." JB spoke up after witnessing his cousin take his last breath.

"Man, I almost don't wanna kill you. But since I killed your cousin, you will most likely come for a nigga head, so you gotta go, Foolie," Fatts said and took him out the game.

$$$$

I pulled into the lot a little earlier than planned to meet up with the crazy bitch. My dick game is boss but damn this bitch willing to drop a few stacks on a nigga just to put the dick on her. I hope Zyyah's ass don't be trippin' like that.

Walking up the back entrance to stay under the radar, I sent a quick text to my inside connect to let me in. My homie hooked me up with the undetected route and a housekeeping key because I felt a little leary by this whole meeting. There were just so many different tones in the text messages we had been sending, I had to take precaution.

215

Click.

I let myself into the room and it seemed desolate. The lights were dim, there were rose petals all over the bed and floor, with candles everywhere. "Talk about savor the moment," I spoke a little above a whisper. Sade's *Ordinary Love* was playing softly with the shower water running in the bat'rum. The closer I got to the bed, I realized there was money and a note. Grabbing the note, I started reading it, then I felt a cold piece of steel on the back of my dome.

Click. I heard the hammer hit the emptiness of the chamber against the back of my head. "Next one ain't gone be that sweet, my boy," a male voice boasted from behind me.

"Man, who the fuck is you, ya heard me. This some sick ass shit, the fuck kind of games you playin, my nigga?"

"I'm Faye's husband nigga, it was me who baited you here. I been knowing about you fucking my wife for a minute now. I was ok with doing whatever and accepting her infidelity, as long as she came home happy every night. It was all good until you told her y'all couldn't be together no more unless she got a divorce," this fuck nigga said.

"She's in love with you nigga, it's no longer about the sex that she moaned about in her sleep. You fucking up my hustle. Turn the fuck around and face your maker nigga," I spun around with a grimace on my face, but burst into laughter.

"Nigga, you came to murder me with fuckin' slacks and Kenneth Cole's on? Is you serious right now, bruh?" I laughed even harder. "But for real, for real, that's between you and yo bitch; check her ass about this shit, ya heard me. Maybe if you was hittin' it right my nigga, me and all the other niggas she fuckin' wouldn't be a factor. Weak and whack! Ahhhhh!"

Reaching back with all his might, he slapped me with the pistol across the left side of my face. "Is that all ya pussy ass got, man? I know a bitch name Sharome that hit harder than you!" I laughed even harder, unfazed and unbothered.

"Nigga, you think I'm one of these lil' young niggas out chere? I'm forty-years-old, I don't play pussy games with bucks," he cocked his gun, heated and I still had a stone face.

"Blah, blah, fuckin blah. My nigga, save the bullshit cuz I don't give a fuck how old you is." *Ptt.* I spit on the nigga shoe.

"Nigga these is hundred-and-forty-dollar shoes. That was disrespectful, I got something special for your ass!" he was livid over me spitting on them cheap ass shoes. My cologne cost more than that shit.

Moments later…

"Bruh, why you got me on the fuckin' roof. I like the view and all but damn, it ain't this serious," the stupid ass nigga didn't even take my heater. Honestly, he didn't check to see if I had one. It's O-V for his duck ass. "Bruh, you that mad about a nigga spitting on them cheap ass shoes or that mad about a nigga dicking down ya no walls having ass wife?"

217

"Don't speak ill about my Faye, you will die a slow death fucking with her character," he defended.

"What character, the only role she play is being your wife, fuck ass nigga. I'm sure every one of my guys done fucked her for a stack," I laughed, further pissing him off. The nigga's chest heaved up and down like a five-year-old. "Oh, I see you mad. You say you a forty-year-old man, put ya heat down and fight me like a man, my nigga." He contemplated on that gesture. "So you scared or nah, lil' bitch?"

Strategically placing his pistol on the ground, he charged me. By him being a tiny might in comparison to my stature, I stood my ground and grabbed his fuck ass by the throat and dug into his esophagus. He gasped for air, like his punk ass came up from the water. I took the concealed pistol from my waist, and crashed the butt of my forever bitch into his nut sack.

He was crying, gasping, and faintly screaming in excruciating pain. "Man, you should've stayed your old ass home tonight and watched reruns of *The Young and the Restless*. Since we are done playing around, I need to be somewhere. You were done, right?" I asked, and he nodded his head. I gave him a helping hand, because I'm Kez, why wouldn't I?

We headed back around to the door that would bring us to the inside of the hotel. He moaned in pain as he walked. I placed my arm around his shoulder as we got to the ledge near the entrance.

"Was she really worth it?" I whispered.

His eyes got big as silver dollars as I took two big steps and launched him over the side of the building. I got out of there in lightning speed, exiting the same way I entered. I headed to my car undetected.

Chapter 27 – Faith

These niggas think they just gone turn twin against me? We was happy before y'all came into the picture, now this nigga tryna leave to go to Arizona for a better life. The fuck he mean he wanted to be a lawyer. I knew he talked about the shit, but that nigga didn't have to go across the country. He could go to Loyola or LSU. He could even go to Southern, they got a lot of fine bitches there. It's an HBCU, I might even enroll in Pimpology.

"Big Twin, you really finna leave me?" I asked Hope as he packed his last bag.

"Yup." Was all he said.

"The fuck I'm supposed to do?"

"Don't know, don't care," Hope responded.

"The fuck you mean you don't care?" I yelled and ran up to him.

"Just what I said, Twin. I'm tired of all this hoe shit you doing to prove a point to ya bitch ass paw. You wanna talk about Big Sissy don't give a fuck about us. You are sadly mistaken, it's that nigga that don't give a fuck, ya heard me?" He chested up like he wanted to fight.

"Nigga, you done got all kind of hard since you been hanging around them fuck niggas, huh?" I pushed him on his bed.

He laughed an evil laugh that sent chills down my spine. I hadn't heard that devil since we were kids. It was when he pushed his best friend in the deep end of the pool for showing off.

Big Twin did it knowing he couldn't swim. However, I didn't back down.

"Bruh, don't fuck with me, I wanna do better. In order to change the outcome, you gotta change the income, so get the fuck out my face before you regret it."

"Ooooh, nigga, you is scaring me!" I stepped closer into his personal space.

"Look, either you gonna let me leave in peace so we can remain cool or, I'mma fuck you up in ya and we will be distant relatives." That shit cut me like razor blades. "I have made a lot of mistakes, but it's time for me to right my wrongs. I wanna do something major with my life and if you don't want to be a part of that, there's nothing I can do to change it," I looked at him like he had two heads.

"Bruh, if you don't get the fuck on with that soft ass shit!" Raising my hand to push him again, he grabbed my wrist.

"I told you to keep ya fucking hands off me, Lil' Twin. If you don't want to be shit, that's on you, son. I have forgiven myself for all the fuck ups, up until now. It is time to change, my dude," he pushed my arm away from his body. "Forgiveness is nothing but recognizing the reality of what has happened has already happened, and there's no point in allowing it to dominate or dictate the rest of your life."

"Nigga you ain't Donatello, tryna spit poetry and shit."

"Bitch, it's Raphael. You got the wrong Ninja Turtle, stupid ass." We both laughed. I couldn't hate on him for wanting better, I just hated that he was leaving me to get it. "Law school, brother? I'm out chere chasing the bag but my nigga say he chasing the whole bank, huh?"

"Nah, nigga, I want the whole Wall Street!" He gut-punched me, which onset a wrestling match. After a few minutes, he laid across his bed and I sat at his computer desk to catch my breath.

"I'mma miss you, big bro. How long is that program again?" I queried.

$$$$

After helping Big Twin load up the Navigator with his shit, I checked my tracker to see where Kez bitch ass was located. "I'mma be right back, ya heard me?" I let Hope know I was leaving.

"Bruh, don't be gone all night. You know I'm dipping at five a.m." he warned. "You know what, just show a nigga some love right now. I know how you get when you get with the hoe of the night," he laughed.

"Who said I was going fuck with some hoes? I'll fuck with you later, my nigga, I'mma be back fo you leave," I winked at him and headed out.

Arriving to my destination in no time, I noticed three cars parked outside. Good thing I was able to fuck the shit outta the bitch at Enterprise, she bit the bait. Hoes do stupid ass shit for that *good wood*. Glad to be a nigga, the giver and not the receiver. I parked across the street where there were several cars so that I wouldn't stick out like a sore thumb. When he pulled out I followed him close enough to still be incognito. It wasn't necessary to stay on his ass because I had a tracker on his rental.

Sitting in my car, I took notice to several vehicles coming and going. I sat so long, I started to get tired. "I wonder if his bitch know that he meeting somebody at a hotel? A nice one at that..." I spoke to myself inside of my car. I started playing Candy Crush on my phone cuz a nigga was bored.

I had played for so long and was so engaged, I almost missed him. I looked up just in time. *I got that fuck nigga now. It was lights out for his bitch ass, he ain't off my blocks yet. He finna be laid to rest,* I thought to myself as I saw Jacques exit the back door of the hotel. Noticing all of the commotion that was popping off, I knew it was gonna be an easy lick. I checked my gun and pulled the hammer back, putting one in the chamber, I exited my car and headed in the direction of my arch nemesis. Within a few feet of him I felt a cold piece of steel to the back of my head. Mere seconds later, a rag was placed over my nose. *Fuck, it was lights out!*

Moments Later...

Splash.

Those niggas woke me up with a bucket of water to my face. Opening my eyes, everything was blurry. Once I regained my sight and caught my breath, I notice a dude tied up across from me. He was fucked up. His face was blue and purple, his eyes were shut, and his mouth leaked so much blood, I didn't understand how he was still breathing.

The slits of his eyes opened, it was like I was looking into my soul. As I looked beyond the swelling, I knew that he was familiar… TWIN!!!

Chapter 28 – Jap

"What's up fellas, I'm glad to have both my future brother-in-laws in the same room. I need to set some ground rules before I marry ya sister," I smiled. Fatts had messed one of them boys up. Looking at the scratch under Fatts' eye, it was obvious he tried to fight. Anybody in their right mind know not to fight that long ass nigga. It made for a good ass whooping and a night of torture, being that he was the king of it.

"What the fuck y'all niggas did to my brother, man? He didn't want no parts of this shit," the fish out of water screamed at the top of his lungs. Those cries fell on deaf ears.

"He shouldn't have tried to fight, I was just gonna K.O. his ass and bring him here in one piece," Fatts laughed. "I asked him if he wanted to do it the easy way or the hard way and he thought he was hard. Ahhhhh!" Still laughing at his own joke, I scowled at him.

"So you must be the infamous Faith?" I queried.

"Yeah bitch, I'm Faith. You fucked up when you came for my twin."

"Nah, lil' one. You fucked up when you came for your sister. Not once but twice, bitch nigga," I slapped him so hard, his neck cracked. He glared at me with a sinister grin on his face.

"I'm addicted to pain, ya heard me. Fuck you and yo' bitch. She is a spawn of Sin just like we are. It won't be long before you find out her true colors," he spat blood in my face.

"That attitude is why we in this predicament right now, Lil' Twin. We are captives and you still talking cash money shit. Bruh, just shut the fuck up. I swuh mane, if I wasn't tied up, I would fuck you up." I was in awe. It was like I was watching a replay of me and Kez, but the twin episode.

"The lil' nigga did say he was off to Tucson for prelaw, Big Foolie. I thought his fuck ass was lying to a nigga for empathy. Plus, I didn't know it was really him. I mean even if I did, it wouldn't have made a difference. His bitch ass would still be here," Fatts chimed in.

"When I get loose, I'm gone knock both of y'all niggas out just like I did to ya pussy ass brother Kez. That nigga so arr-, arro-, full of hisself that I just had to give his fuck ass a concussion."

"Arrogant is the word. Nigga, you dumb as fuck. You definitely the nigga who left that note with your illiterate ass," Fatts said. Walking over to the twin, now known to be Faith, he slapped the slob out of his mouth. Hitting him with an uppercut to the chin he smiled. "That's for spitting on my round, bitch nigga!"

"Ahhhhh!" he laughed again. I don't know why that nigga was so damn goofy.

I walked around tapping my forehead and chewing the inside of my cheek. It was something I had been known to do since I was a kid. For some odd reason, it allowed me to clear my thoughts to make a decision.

"Okay, here's what I'm gonna do. I'm not gonna kill y'all niggas today, because even though y'all don't know her, Chyna loves y'all. So on the strength of her, I have come to this conclusion," I paused, almost feeling sorry for Hope. He actually told the truth about wanting nothing to do with the bullshit and going away to school.

"What's waiting in the wings on the other side of this door is far worse than what either of us had planned to do to you," I finished.

"Tuh, I had planned to torture Faith. Hope, I may have let you live, in a wheelchair," Fatts chimed in.

"Only one of you will survive. Once me and my lil' one ya, make it to the door, I'mma slide in a pistol. Y'all gone have to choose between who lives and who dies," I spoke my truth.

"What the fuck man, that shit ain't fair," Faith yelled.

"I can't kill my brother so, I guess I'm dead," Hope admitted. "Are you going to untie us?" he asked.

"Nah, son. That would be too much. Knowing Sin, and the fact that you two are his offspring, y'all might try to shoot us in the backs. With that being said, y'all have two choices... Die in this cold room together or figure out how to untie each other so one of y'all can be bait and the other one can escape."

"That's pretty damn clever. You right, Big Foolie, it's far worse than what I had planned," Fatts admitted while rubbing his goatee.

"What's on the other side of the door?" Hope enquired with wide eyes.

"I'm glad you asked," I opened the door. *Whooort*, I whistled, and a huge pit bull came running in. "This ya is Queen. She's smaller than her brothers, weighing in at one hundred forty-three pounds. They are trained to attack anyone that they aren't familiar with. Go say hi Queen," she walked up to Faith and got nose-to-nose then growled.

He literally pissed his pants causing her to lick his urine from between his legs. "Enough, go say hi to the other one." Walking over to Hope, she got in his face and found his eyes. I swear she had empathy for him. Maybe he was a good kid. *Whooort* "Let's go, Queen," she walked out, taking one last growl at Faith.

"The ball is in your court now. Since y'all like games and shit, y'all can play the devil's advocate, and choose each other's fate. AM I MY BROTHER'S KEEPER?" I yelled emptying the gun clip of all but three bullets and sliding it against the wall. "Deuces, dog meat."

Chapter 29 – Zyyah

It had been three weeks since Jacques had taken me to Gulf Shores. I was surprised that he stuck around. He had such a tough exterior that I assumed he would be the epitome of 'hitting it and quitting it.' We had been spending so much time together, I almost thought we were a couple. I dug his style so a great deal. The little mystery in him had no effect on whatever the thing between us was.

Sitting at the Louis Armstrong International Airport awaiting my Bestie's arrival, had me nervous. Sure, she had spoken to Jacques over the phone and sent her empty threats about hurting me, but this was the real deal. They would finally meet face-to-face, I had a feeling they would bump heads because she was a fire cracker, and he, a hot head. Her flight had landed about ten minutes ago, she should've been walking up any minute.

"Shucks, now I have to waste my gas," I spoke to my rearview mirror. Those stupid airport security guards are far worse than the ones at Sky Harbor. It was like they were waiting in the shadows to catch you sitting so they could have a reason to have an attitude about making you move your car. "No waiting," I mocked as she reached the tail end of my car. I didn't wait for her to make it to the window, I pulled off.

No sooner than I got back in line, my phone rang. Checking the caller ID, I saw that it was Deja and answered. "Agggggh! Best, you finally touched down," I yelled.

"Si amiga (yes, friend), donde estas (where are you)? It's humid out here and it's is fucking with my mane!" she yelled in Spanglish.

"I'm right here, looking at you D.Q., you need to stop cutting up already. I'm pulling up now." She was too much for TV and definitely too much for what I had in store for her behind. I pulled up and got out to help her with her bags. She kept eyeing me like she was trying to read me.

"Girl, why do you keep looking at me crazy?" I quizzed.

"I'm trying to figure out what hit you and your bank account. You didn't tell me you got a new car, bitch. You only told me about one of your new rides, and it has legs. Spill, whore," she hit my arm. She was so touchy, it drove me crazy at times.

"Girl bye, this is a rental. Jacques put my car in the shop because it was overdue on everything. He also wanted to get a fresh paint job."

"Zaaaaaam bitch, I need me a Jacques," she said, and I cut my eyes at her. "You have a sponsor, why can't I have one?" She was serious.

"I don't have a sponsor, so don't come for me. I pay my own way. He asked could he give me an early birthday gift and of course I said yes. I had no idea it would be to that extreme."

Quickly catching an attitude, Deja knew that I had never been a gold digger.

"Tuh, you got a lil' dick and suddenly a lot of sauce, huh Best. I'm just gonna be quiet, cuz you think you so 504, you might try to catch a fade if I say the wrong thing."

"You know that I would never try to fight you, but you also know that I get defensive when it comes to my independence. To get off of this subject, I'm glad you came dressed cute," I cleared the air.

"Why?" She questioned hesitantly.

"Because we were invited to a birthday dinner at Bobby Hebert's. Since you look cute, we don't have to drive all the way to the East so you can get dressed."

"Bobby Hebert's, like where all of the ballers are? You know I'm in." I swear she is my best friend. Her thirsty, man-eating ways are not ladylike. I couldn't judge her though, because I love her.

We talked for a while as we got out of the airport traffic and headed to the restaurant. I told her about the people who would be in attendance and she already had it out for Chyna. Over the past month, Chy and I had gotten pretty close and De didn't like the fact that I had another friend. She felt her place in my life would be taken.

It was like we were kids all over again. She had friends galore, but I could only have one friend, and that was her. That always made me feel like she kept me around as the "ugly duckling". I was never ugly, but I was always the thicker one of the group, which made most guys flock to her and her skinny friends, leaving me as a fifth wheel. Most people wondered why I still hung out with her, the reason being she never made me feel like I wasn't loved. She has never treated me indifferent, she always uplifted me. I guess I was more self-conscious than anything.

Pulling into the parking lot of the restaurant, Deja flopped the mirror down and freshened up her make-up. Me, on the other hand, I was more comfortable in my own skin. I added a small amount of lip gloss. We winked at each other, alerting one another that we were good to go. It was something we had done since we were around thirteen.

Walking into the establishment, we headed towards the back where the dinner party was. No sooner than we walked in, Deja started asking questions about who was who. "Oooh Best, you know I'm not into the light-skinned guys, but who is that looking this way licking his lips?" She was in full-blown lust mode. I mean Jacques and all of his homeboys were eye candy but, her thing was chocolate men.

"I have not a clue, Bestie," I lied, just wanting to see how far she'd take it. "He is sexy though, right?" I smiled back.

"OMG, Best, he is coming this way. How do I look? I'm bout to be his snack for the night," she said excitedly.

"I don't do snacks, baby. I do full course meals, ya heard me. Ain't that right, bae?" he said just loud enough for the two of us to hear. Jacques place a very sensuous kiss on my lips.

"Ugh, get a room, bro," Ju'an teased.

The look on De's face was inexplainable. I didn't know if I should've been upset, hurt, or surprised that she looked like she wanted to leave. She couldn't have been embarrassed, or could she have?

"I'm going to the restroom, sis. I'll be right back," she walked off without waiting for a response.

I, of course, went after her. "Hey, what's your problem?" I inquired once we made it inside of the restroom.

"You made me look like a fool out there." She was so furious, her skin turned crimson red.

"What the heck do you mean, I made you look like a fool?" I rebutted.

"You knew I didn't have a chance with him and you allowed me to flirt. You purposely set me up so that I wouldn't have a chance with any of his homeboys."

"Wait a minute, De, I never set you up. I would never do that to you. You assumed he was coming your way. If anything, you set yourself up by assuming. You are so use to being the pick between the two of us that you just knew he was headed in your direction." It was my turn to be upset, I turned to walk out.

"Sis, wait."

"What is it?" I queried with a slight attitude.

"I'm sorry. I did assume your man was interested in me, and I'm not too grown to apologize," she looked to me with puppy eyes. "Hug?"

Feeling like she was sincere in her apology, I hugged her. We walked back out together and joined the party. After introducing her to everyone, I sat in the corner and caked it up with my baby. Jacques and I had been in each other's company so often that us being together started to feel naturally comfortable. We had been spending nights at each other's houses and going to the movies often. Our once a week dates on the Lakefront were amazing.

A few days later…

"I can't believe you gotta work today, it's my third day here. I'm here on vacation and you didn't take the time off," Deja complained.

"Best, I don't have vacation days. When you leave, I'll have bills to pay. The shift is only six hours, you'll be fine. Go explore. I'll see you in a few hours, boo," I headed out to work and felt bad because of my poor planning.

"Hi Jack, how are you today?" I spoke to my manager with the same cheery smile that I've always greeted him with. Walking to the back of the building to clock in, he interrupted me.

"Zyyah, we've been really slow today. I feel like the census won't pick up much. I know you just got here, but if you wanna go home, it won't be held against your attendance," he stared at me waiting for an answer.

Since I've been in New Orleans, I have learned so much about their culture. The one thing that still amazes me, is the dialect of English here. No matter what race, color, or creed, they all sounded the same.

"Sha, why are you smiling and staring like a creep? Do you or don't you wanna go home? If you don't, I can ask someone else to go," he broke my thoughts.

"Yes, Jack, I'll go. I have out-of-town guests anyway."

Walking back out to my car, I noticed a woman walking briskly from the area where my car was parked. I paid no extra attention because there were two other cars parked near mine.

I made it to my car and noticed a piece of paper stuck in between the wiper blade and the windshield.

STAY AWAY FROM JACQUES OR ELSE BITCH!

Getting into my car, I sat there muddled. I snapped a picture and sent it to Jacques, feeling like he was the only one who could explain.

Chapter 30 – Deja

"I can't believe you took off for the rest of the day to spend time with little old me," I smiled at my best friend.

"I felt bad, sis. You came all the way here to spend time with me. Because of my poor planning or lack thereof, I would've had literally two days to spend with you undisturbed," Zy responded.

"Ok, I'll let you have that." She side-eyed me.

"What do you mean?" Zyyah asked.

"I've known you for the better part of our lives. You're hiding something, but, I'll allow you to tell me in your time. Just know that I'm here, if and when you need or want to talk. Ok? Love you," she gave me a weak smile. I haven't seen Zy that defeated since she quit the music program in college. I felt really sad for her, but I didn't want to force her.

"I love you more, boo."

"Why are you staring at your phone and not answering?" I questioned.

"I don't feel like being bothered right now," Zy responded.

"Lies Bestie, but ok," I said.

"Anyway, what do you wanna do today?"

"Didn't Chyna mention Dubai? Let's go shopping for that, you know I love shopping!"

"I don't think I wanna go to Dubai with them," was all she said.

"Let's go eat some crawdads."

"It's not crawdads, it's crawfish. Ha. Ha."

"Ok Miss 5-0-4. Let's get crawfish and since you're an expert, you can teach me how to eat them."

"Wish I could, but it's not crawfish season soooooo, we can only go to some of the local spots and get crawfish dishes," she schooled me.

"What's a crawfish dish?" I asked.

"Like crawfish pie, étouffée, stew, pasta, etcetera."

"Ok. Well enough is enough. What's up with you and Mr. Jacques?"

"There's nothing up with him and I. I'm over him, I got what I wanted, and I'm done." Zy was talking crazily. Her phone rang, and she hit ignore for what seemed like the hundredth time. "Let's get outta here, please," she requested, not wanting to discuss whatever was on her mind and I didn't press the issue.

"Vamonos (let's go)!"

Chapter 31 – Jacques

Zyyah bailed on me for Dubai without good reason. She had been real distant since we returned. I'm going over to her house and demand answers. It was March and I had seen her maybe three times since we made it back. I told her that I didn't know who would want to put that dumb ass note on her car. Truthfully, I knew it was Faye's bitch ass. I sent that hoe a message letting her know, if she messed with Zy one more time, it was over for her.

Feeling that I needed to see Zy, I sent her a text.

Me: Bae I'm bout 2 come over.

Message read: 8:16 p.m.

Bae: You can come over if you want, but I really don't feel like any company

Message received: 8:18 p.m.

Me: OMW (kissy face)

Message read: 8:19 p.m.

I grabbed my keys and headed out, ready to hold my baby all night. I had missed her thick ass and she was trippin'. I understood how she felt, but it's been almost two months. Just as I locked up and hit the alarm on Pearl, I heard a very familiar voice behind me.

"My husband committed suicide," Faye informed me.

"Do it look like I give a fuck?" I returned with a scowl on my face.

"We can be together now, I don't have to report to anyone. He left me a hefty insurance policy. I can take care of you like you need to be tooken care of," she told me.

"First of all, you are illiterate as fuck. Tooken isn't a word," I got that one from my baby. I used that like no tomorrow. My baby said she wasn't gone have me out chere looking foolish. "What makes you think that I wanna be with your loose ass?"

"I'm beautiful, I'm rich, and I'm willing to do everything to keep my man. I'm a ten," she said, and I thought it was hilarious. I laughed so hard I had tears in my eyes.

"You can start by doing Kegels to tighten that loose ass pussy up."

"Why do you talk to me so bad? It's like you don't love me anymore. I bet you don't talk to that waitress like this. I'm a fucking ten Ja-Ja, and you know it," she called out.

"Bitch, what you mean 'no more'? You is fuckin delusional. When have a nigga ever told you I loved you? I'll wait," I paused. "And for the record, don't kid yourself, community pussy. You might be a ten in the looks department, but my muthafuckin' girl is one in a million, hoe. If you put another note on her car, it's over for you!" I let her funky ass know the real in person since I had previously sent her a text.

Running up to me wrapping her arms around my waist, I tried to get her off me. "Faye, get the fuck up off me, bruh. This ain't what's up. Find a nigga that will love and respect you, cuz it ain't me, ya heard me," I finally was able to push her off.

"I hate you, you motherfucker!" she screamed and started attacking me. She was punching and scratching my arms.

I grabbed her arms and pinned her back against my truck. "Chill the fuck out, bruh. You trippin', ya heard me. I'mma let you go but don't put your fuckin' hands on me no more. Is that shit understood?" She nodded her head. "Nah, I need to hear a confirmation with ya stupid, duck ass," I demanded.

"I'm good, Ja-Ja." No sooner than I let her go she hauled off and smacked me in the face, causing me to choke her ass out.

Once she started to gasp for air, I let her down. "Now get the fuck from round me and don't ever put ya fuckin hands on me again, dumb ass hoe." With that she finally left.

Going back inside of my house, I packed a bag and changed clothes. I wouldn't be coming back to this house for a while. Now that this psycho bitch knows where I laid my head, I could foresee trouble. Finally ready, I headed out towards Zyyah's.

I made it to my baby's house in no time. Parking my truck two buildings down, I walked up to her door and knocked. Hearing the knobs unlock, my heart started to race. When I walked in, she had on this lil' booty shorts sleeping set and I watched that ass all the way to the sofa before closing and locking the door behind me.

"What's up, bae?"

"Nothing, watching *Private Practice* since I finally caught up on Grey's," she had a little bit of attitude.

"Bae, I had a bad day. I didn't come over here for this bullshit. I need solace and I assumed I could get it here."

"Hey, don't come in here with your bad day, taking it out on me because I'm that bitch right now, Jacques," she returned fire. She was no longer my meek little Zyyah. I could tell that that note had fucked with her bad. "You will not enter my apartment being disrespectful. You can get out the same way you came in," she looked at me with hard eyes and flaring nostrils. Damn she was sexy when she was mad, I wondered what that mad pussy was like.

"I apologize, bae, you right. Give me a kiss," she pecked my lips. "Hell naw, give me a kiss bae. Stop playing," I pinched her side, causing her to giggle. I knew I was winning with that, she gave me some tongue action. "So what's this show about?"

"I think you'd like it. Do you remember Derrick's ex-wife, Addison?" she asked.

"Yeah, the one that fucked Sloan…,"

"Why must your mouth be so dirty? But yeah, her. Well Addison goes to California to help Sam Bennett, portrayed by Taye Diggs, and his wife, Naomi, with their practice."

"So, it's like Grey's but a practice instead of a hospital?" I asked.

"Yeah, but they still go to work in the hospital and from what I've read, Naomi becomes their competition."

"Wait, did you read the whole thing on wiki?" I looked at her with my lips poked to the side and my chin up, causing her to laugh.

"No, silly. I read the reviews."

"What season is this?"

"Which season, bae?" she corrected. I didn't mind, it was making me a better-spoken man. "I'm only on season one, episode three. If you want to, we can watch from the beginning. That way you'll understand the backstory." She was considerate.

Laying my head in her lap, her freshness and the pheromones radiating from her vagina had me in a trance. I wasn't able to focus on the show. One thing led to another and before I knew it, I had Zy's juices all over my face.

Chapter 32 – Zyyah

Months later…

Kez and I made things better over the last few months. Things had been going well. We had a ball shopping for Chyna's shower that I hosted at Jacques' house. He invited her and Ju'an over for dinner and surprised her. She, of course, allowed the river to flow. Deja even flew in to help me with it, which was a shocker.

Headed to work in the midday traffic was always a headache. The City was forever working on the interstate at some point and it was ALWAYS in my route of travel. I made it into work on time, for a change. I despised the midday shifts because of the plethora of cars in whichever route I decided to travel. It seemed we all would get off of the interstate within miles of one another, congesting the streets.

I had had a great shift and was placing my last order for a patron when my supervisor approached me. "Zyyah, there's a woman requesting your presence," Jack informed me, just as I placed my ticket in the window for the chef.

"Really?" I questioned curiously. "Is she sitting in my section?"

"No. I don't have time for twenty-one questions, Zyyah. Go take care of your visitor so you can get back to work. Oh, and tell your little friends that this is your job, not a place to socialize," Jack reminded me.

"Hi, how may I help you?" I asked the mystery person.

"So you Zeyah, huh?" she asked.

"Yes, I'm Zyyah. How may I help you?" She was beautiful, but her face showed much distress.

"Oh, you're respectful for a bitch that comfortably sleeps with a woman's husband," she feigned a smile.

"I'm sorry?" I stated confused.

"Bitch, you are definitely sorry. Sleeping with a married man," she yelled.

"I think you got the wrong person. You keep saying that I'm sleeping with a married man. I'm not real sure about what you mean."

"Bitch, you know what I mean, don't insult me," she yelled louder than she did the first time. "I'm only going to say this once, Jacques Anderson is mine. I have worked too hard to groom him into the man that I wanted him to be and I will not lose him to a bitch like you," she flashed her wedding ring. "Ha. Judging by the look on your face, you must've been under the impression that you were his one and only. No bitch, you are a side chick. I am his number one and he will never leave me. I'm Mrs. Faye Anderson, you and no other hoe will change that." She looked so evil.

I was speechless, the people of the restaurant stared in our direction. She came to my job and embarrassed me.

"Oh bitch, the cat got your tongue? Do you not have shit to say, you homewrecking hoe?" She pulled out a switch blade and lunged towards me, causing me to side step and land my strong fist into her cheek. It must have been a lucky hit, because she was laid out cold on the floor.

Gasps of the restaurant attendees could be heard from every direction.

"Home-wrecking whore! She should've cut you," someone yelled out in blind judgement.

"Zyyah, you're fired. Regardless to who started what, we will not have this kind of unruliness taking place in our establishment."

"But Jack, I don't know this woman. I need my job. Please," I cried as the police showed up.

"Ma'am, can we speak to you please?" the police asked. I obliged like a law-abiding citizen. I mean, it wasn't as if I could say no, so I stepped outside to talk with them. I have not been this embarrassed since I was removed from class by the police for a disagreement with a teacher and her daughter.

After everything was said and done, I left with fire in my eyes. I never wanted to see his lying face again. I had found the clippings of Pita and he was open about what happened, it didn't sit well with me, but I swallowed it. He told me about his relationship with his mother and how she was only in his pockets, but because he loved her, he allowed it. I was ok with that.

He had no idea who his father was, therefore he had no male guidance other than Ju'an's dad. Of course, there were several men in and out of his life. They beat his mother and abused him every chance they got. I was willing to sit through counseling sessions for that. To be a mistress was one thing I was not willing to be.

Calling Deja on the phone, I was furious.

"Hey, Best," she answered all cheery as usual.

"Hey, I need you here yesterday, I am getting a U-Haul and breaking my lease. It's time for me to come home. New Orleans was a mistake."

"Say no more, I'll be there next week so you can get everything squared away with work and your lease agreement. I love you, sis." was all she said before we hung up. When we were in distress we did what was asked, without question.

Hanging up with her, I called Chyna.

"Hey Sha, what's up? Please don't tell me that you're bailing on the event this weekend," she cringed.

"No, but I'm headed back to Arizona next week. I felt I needed to let you know being that we've established a friendship and please, allow me to tell Jacques," I requested.

"Ok, love," she responded. "Is there something I can do to get you to stay?"

"No, unfortunately. It just isn't working out for me," I replied.

"When are you pulling out?"

"Next Friday morning," I informed her. "I gotta hang up, my father is on the other line. Love you, Pud," I referred to her by a nickname I had given her because she was as lovely to the core as pudding was to the soul.

Chapter 33 – Fatts

Picking the baby shower gift was fun. It was my first time at any kind of event like that. I can't say I wanted any kids anytime soon, though. That shit is expensive and I'm too selfish and stingy. I didn't wanna share my girl or my money with a kid. Hell, I ain't even mad that they picked Jacques as the godfather, which was a given, given the history of him a Jap. I prayed that nothing happened to either of them, but if something did, that meant that I would have to take care of this kid like it was my own.

Zyyah was a cool addition to our lil' family. She really changed Big Foolie in a good way. I hope they last forever cuz that nigga used to be mean as shit. He was definitely a nigga only family could love. Niggas not only respected him, but they feared him. Not me, I'd fight his big ass, but don't tell him I said that. That nigga might try to get the gloves out or some shit, then I would have to K.O. That boy in front of everybody. Ahhhhh! Y'all know I'm the childish, goofy, murderer of the fam. I mean, I was the baby. What else would you expect?

To all of my fans, I know you only had bits and pieces of me throughout this story. However, it's all good, a nigga is about to blow up, finally have some airtime ya heard me. I got my own shit coming out, yep all about me, Toy, and our childhoods. Have your Kleenex ready cuz a nigga been through some shit ya heard me, Foolies!

A nigga bout to be twenty-one, ready for fun. Ahhhhh! We are gonna do it up do it big in my shit, ya heard me. I hope Chy and Casey go all out for my shit like they did for Jap cuz that was amazing. Now that we got my lil' stuff outta the way, I will chat it up with y'all in the next installment. Let y'all see things from my point of view, ya heard me... one hunnit!

Chapter 34 – Faye

"Ja-Ja, what are you doing here?" I asked after I swung my door open, thinking it was the lieutenant, for more questioning about my husband's suicide. It had been months and the fucked-up part was, his insurance policy was void because of the suicide clause. I couldn't say that I wasn't happy to see Jacques.

Opening the door wide enough for him to enter my five-bedroom home, he hesitated. "Is your kid here?"

"No, she is away at cheer camp."

"Perfect," he stated looking around at my beautiful pristine home.

"I see you're a neat freak. I wouldn't have imagined a dirty-pussy bitch to have such a clean home," he smirked making my pussy thump. Every time that dimple peeked through his cheek it did something to me. "The fuck you staring at me like that for? Take a nigga on a tour. Let me see what the pad looks like."

"How did you know where I lived?" I smiled, not wanting to give him any clue that I was going to jab him with a needle to paralyze him and ride his dick. I was having his baby one way or the other.

"The same way you knew where I lived. You ain't the only one that have resources." We toured the whole house and he never removed his hands from his pockets.

"Last but not least, the room where the magic happens. I have a surprise for you, stay here," I warned as I walked into my massive master's closet. I stripped down to nothing, then donned a beautiful, pink and black negligée with full gloves. I threw the gloves on so that I could keep the syringe concealed.

Walking seductively toward him, I took notice of the lust in his eyes as he licked his full lips. He talked all that shit about disliking me, but I knew better. Finally scaring the bitch away from him, *daddy was home*. Just as I made it close enough to him, I was in motion to wrap my arms around his neck, but to no avail.

Grabbing me by the wrist, he slowly backed me into the wall near the closet and whispered in my ear. "What's in the needle, bitch?"

"What needle, Ja-Ja?" I responded, trying to figure out how he knew what I had done.

"The fuckin needle you put in ya left glove, hoe," he looked me in the eye, I swore I seen the devil in them.

"I- I- I don't have a needle in my…," taking notice of his hands for the first time, I trailed off because he was wearing black hospital gloves. "Why are you wearing gloves, baby?"

"Why are you lying about the needle? Did you forget that you had a mirrored door that gave off the reflection of you preparing whatever it was you drew up?" Realizing I fucked up, I had to think fast.

"It's for stamina. I needed to be fucked long and hard, so I figured I would give us the extra push that we needed," I fibbed.

"Ha, ha, ha. Bitch, you crazy as fuck." Finding humor in what I said, he slammed my arms against the wall above my head causing the needle to fall near my feet. "You gotta be fuckin' stupid if you think I'm buying that shit. I ain't neva had no damn problem with lasting in your deep ass pussy," he released my arms turning to walk away.

I kneeled to pick up the needled, then heard a gun being cocked. "Un-un bitch, night, night!" He pulled the trigger, sending a bullet crashing through my skull.

Chapter 35 - Jacques

Man, I fucked up in a major way. This crazy bitch done made a nigga take her and her duck ass husband out of the game, for good. Besides that, I might've lost Zyyah. I haven't heard from her in a hot minute. I couldn't understand how a married bitch would be that psycho over a nigga, it was beside me. I couldn't believe Faye showed up to my girl's job. Me and Zy was doing good. I continued to check my inbox, even though I knew she hadn't text me back, because I fell asleep with my phone in my hand. I looked over the messages I had sent to her in a span of three hours. That shit made me feel like a stalker.

Me: Bae, stop being dramatic and answer your damn phone bruh.

Message read: 8:44 p.m. Yesterday

Me: Bae, don't make me come fuck you up!

Message read: 8:54 p.m. Yesterday

Me: Bae, I promise that bitch ain't a factor no more! I stopped fuckin with her the day after we went to Anita's on our "not first date"

Message read: 9:18 p.m. Yesterday

Me: Fuck man, you gone make me hurt your ass for real, for real!

Message read: 11:44 p.m. Yesterday

I decided to send her ass one last message before I headed over to her crib. She was leaving me on read, she knew how much that shit fucked with my mental. We had been fucking around for about six or seven months, she wanted something I didn't. In the beginning, we was good at being friends with benefits. I knew it pissed me off when she didn't answer or when she wasn't available for me, but, I just felt like I was being selfish because I made time for her. I felt different about our situation-ship, and Jap's bitch ass kept telling me I was in love, but that nigga thought everybody was in love, because he was. Ol' lovey-dovey ass nigga.

> *Me: If you don't answer me, I'm coming to your crib and it ain't gone be nothing decent!*
> *Message sent: 6:39 p.m.*

I had been laying in my funk all evening, so I decided to hop in the shower. After I was all clean and smelling like new money, I hit my sis line cuz a nigga knew she wouldn't steer me wrong. She liked Zy, over time they had become friends, but her loyalty was to me. I was her brother. Picking up my phone, I checked my messages and noticed Zy hadn't opened the message I sent an hour and a half ago. I hit Chyna up. "Hey sis, what you up to?"

"Don't 'what you up to' me, ninja. I'm almost nine months pregnant trying to get your girlfriend to stop loading her U-Haul," Chy yelled into the phone. I was confused like a muthafucka. I grabbed my keys and headed out.

"What the fuck you mean her U-Haul?" I countered back. It had only been a week and she had already packed up and was

ready to bounce out a nigga life because of some simple shit.
"I'm in route sis, don't let her leave!"

"What the hell do you want me to do, Kez? Stand my
whale of an ass in front of a seventeen-foot U-Haul? I think not,
you better get your ass here, and get here fast. She only has one
room left to load!" Chy said.

I heard Deja's ass in the background, she had not too long
ago flown back to Phoenix so, I knew shit was serious.

"Can I speak to him?" Deja asked.

"No De, I don't need you to fight my battles. I'm over it,
he doesn't want to be with me the way I want to be with him and
after last week I know why… He's married, his wife came up to
the restaurant and made it very clear," I heard Zy say in the
background.

"What? Married!" Chyna and Deja yelled in unison.

"She flashed her rock and tried to cut me in the face.
Saying she loved him long before I was ever in the picture and
she wasn't going to lose her husband to a big bitch like me. I was
only a toy for when he was bored. Apparently, he's been playing
on my emotional state the whole time. I had fallen in love with
another woman's husband, I feel like such a fool!" The pain in
Zy's voice as she revealed her encounter with that psycho bitch,
broke my heart.

"Best, why didn't you tell me all of this before today. Ese
hijo de puta, voy a matarlo! (That son of a bitch, I'm going to kill
him)," Deja yelled some shit in Spanish, pissing me off. It only

pissed me off because I couldn't understand. Every time she was around I needed a fuckin translator.

"Ha. Ha. Haaaa," Chyna broke into laughter.

"What's so damn funny, Mrs. Perfect Relationship. I watched you last time I was here, you pretend to love my sister while looking down your nose at her," Deja spat at Chyna. I needed to hurry before sis smacked the fuck outta little Miss Rosie Perez.

"Sha, are you serious? Kez ain't married to nobody but the game!" Chyna informed Zyyah of my truth. "Deja, I'm only gonna say this once. I have never disrespected you and I won't. However, make this your last time talking out the side of your neck to me. You don't know me, and you don't know shit about my relationship. I care about Zy, why the hell do you think I'm here?" Chy was angry.

"Please stop you guys, I have enough going on. De, you were wrong to say those things, you can't take your frustrations out on Chyna. She has nothing to do with the decisions of Jacques," I pulled up to see the shit was true. There was a U-Haul parked in front of Zyyah's apartment building. I ended the call because they had apparently forgot I was on the line.

I parked my Caprice and walked up to the truck as Zy was putting a box in the back. "Baby, what are you doing?" Zy looked at me with red puffy eyes. She shook her head violently.

"No. You don't get to call me baby. Go home to your wife. You made me look like a clown. I trusted you, I opened up my heart and allowed my soul to bleed into yours and you…," she paused as tears rushed down her face. I ran up to her, I just needed a moment to explain everything.

She put her hand out and it landed in the middle of my chest. I can't lie, a nigga felt some type of way. She denied my affection and I couldn't believe it. It took months to break her walls down, and seconds for it to rebuild.

"Bae, I'm not married. I wouldn't do that to you. Hell, if I had a wife, I damn sure wouldn't do it to her," I admitted.

"Wow, so you definitely wouldn't be with *me* if you were married. She was right, I was a toy that you played with and put back on the shelf, whenever the fuck you felt like it." As long as we had been messing around, I only heard her cuss in the bedroom. She was pissed.

"C'mon nah Z, you know damn well that ain't what I meant. Don't fuckin' put words in my mouth."

By that time, we had an audience. Chyna stood there crying with her emotional ass and of course, Deja fuck ass stood there staring at me like she wanted to kill me. That bitch coulda tried it. "Z, please let me explain baby!"

"Don't fall for that caca (shit) falling from his boca de mentira (lying mouth) mi hija (girl)," Deja's instigating ass was driving me nuts in English and Spanish.

"Can you just be quiet for a second, J-Lo, and let her think for herself?" I looked at her so evil, I felt the frown lines forming on my forehead.

"Baby, listen to me. Just because my eyes don't tear, it don't mean my heart don't cry. I didn't imagine my life with a woman because of things you already know about. But now that you are trying to walk away, I can't imagine my life without you. I love you, baby, and I'm ready to make this shit official," I looked Zy in the eyes and never missed a beat. She stared at me with tears streaming down her face. At that moment, I was afraid that I didn't get through to her.

I didn't pray until I needed to get out of a jam. I found myself praying to get into something; Zyyah's heart. I needed her heart to feel mine, so she could feel me rather than hear me. I grabbed her face and kissed her with every ounce of passion that I had ever felt. A passion that I didn't know I had. She wept. When we came up for air, she closed the door to the U-Haul.

"You broke me, Jacques. All I wanted to do was love you. We spent a lot of time together and you never once mentioned a wife. I'm no one's second choice. When you get your ducks in a row, you'll be able to find me in Arizona. I won't wait forever. Let's go, De."

"Don't explain shit to him, you don't owe anyone an explanation. Fuck that nigga," Deja spat towards me.

"Who the fuck asked you? Why don't you shut your punk ass up, I'm tired of you," I spat making Deja cower.

"Don't speak to her that way. If you disrespect her, you will disrespect me and we both know I don't play those games," Zy checked me.

"This shit right here is why we wouldn't work anyway. You don't pick your friend over your man. Just go ahead and hit that slab. I won't lose any sleep. Have a safe trip, ya heard me!" With that a lone tear escaped her eye. I could say that it didn't disturb me but if I can be honest, that shit broke my heart.

"You're not my man, remember. You didn't want to put a title on things. Have a nice life, Jacques. You're right, this would have never worked," she motioned her hand between us. She got in the truck and they pulled off.

"Kez, what is wrong with you? That girl loves you and judging by the brokenness in your eyes, you love her too. Don't let your pride allow you to lose your soulmate. When it is meant to be, if it's one day or ten years, you'll know. Matters of the heart doesn't include other people's opinions. If you don't go after her, I feel like you'll lose more than you'll gain," Chy scolded me like a true big sister would.

"Sis, what do I do now? I never felt so lost." A real nigga cried a real tear. Chy came up to me and hugged me. I fucked up.

"First, call the private investigator to find out where her parents live. Then call our travel agent to book the first flight to Phoenix. But right now, I'mma need you to suck that shit up and get me to the hospital cuz my water just broke fucking with y'all and this Thug Story!"

To my fans and supporters,

Thank you for riding with me on this journey. I stepped out on faith and through all of my trials, here we are on book two. I hope you have enjoyed this read as much as I enjoyed writing it. Book three will be following this one much closer, than two followed book one.

Book three is Fatts and LaToy's Thug story. They have been through a storm to get in the headspace that they were in in the previous stories. You will laugh, cry, get angry, and possibly cry some more. There was a plethora of emotions poured on each of those pages.

Also, if you would like to be a character visual in any of my upcoming stories, inbox me a photo, name of the character, and the growth of the character. There is no monetary reward for it, however, your face will float around social media allowing you to become someone's book bae.

Again, I'm just a girl from New Orleans, LA trying to live my best life. Stick around to be a part of these amazing stories. Thanks for riding with me.

To contact me through social media, here are my accounts:

Facebook: D'Ashanta's Fans and Beyond, Shhhh! I'm Reading reader's group, and Desaree Authoress D'Ashanta Jackson personal page.

Instagram: @just_desaree

Twitter: Authoress D'Ashanta @desareej

Also from Allure Me Presents:

D'Ashanta

A Thug's Story Not a Love Story 1

Evelyn Latrice

Block Boyz and the Women That Cuff Them

Loving a Young Rich Savage 1-2

From the Depths of My Soul 1-3

Trappin': Love On The Come Up w/ Mesha Mesh

Dominique Nikail

Foolishly in Love with You

Queen Ki

The Streets Made Me a Savage, She Made Me a King 1-2

Dani Lane

Before You Cross Me

CPSIA information can be obtained
at www.ICGtesting.com
Printed in the USA
LVHW03s2108200618
581394LV00001B/55/P

9 781987 534283